# SYLVIA MERCEDES

## THE VENATRIX CHRONICLES BOOK 4

© 2020 by Sylvia Mercedes

Published by FireWyrm Books

www.SylviaMercedesBooks.com

Cover design by Deranged Doctor Design

*This one is for you, Esther,*
*Since you said it was your favorite.*

Drauval Borough

Skada Mountains

Aalis River

Castra Brecar

Wodechran

Sang River

Tehanor City

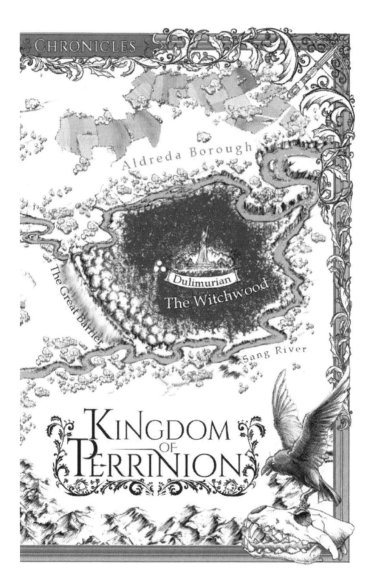

CHRONICLES

Aldreda Borough

The Great Barrier

Dulimurian

The Witchwood

Sang River

KINGDOM
OF
PERRINION

THE VENATRIX

Aalis River

Rivanduru

Carduru

Höllen

Elsinoe

Dunloch Castle

Milisendis

Cabralet

WODECHRAN
BOROUGH

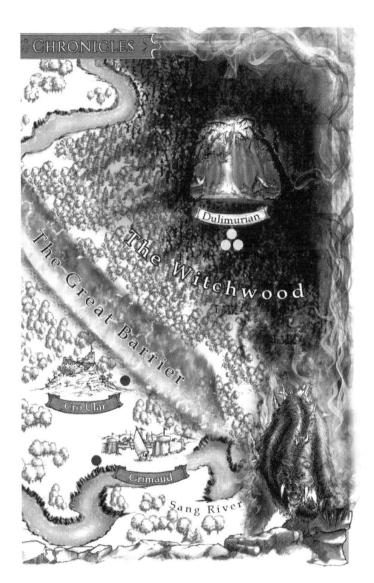

Dulimurian

The Witchwood

The Great Barrier

Cro Ular

Grimaud

Sang River

# GLOSSARY OF SHADES

**Shades:** Disembodied spirit-beings who have escaped from their hellish dimension—the Haunts—and entered the mortal world. They cannot exist in a physical reality without mortal hosts, whom they possess and endow with unnatural powers. If left unchecked, they will gain ascendancy within a host-body and oust the original soul, taking full possession.

The following are the known varieties of shades as catalogued by the Order of Saint Evander:

## ANATHEMAS
Abilities pertain to blood and curse-casting.

## APPARITIONS
Abilities pertain to mind control and manipulation.

## ARCANES
Mysterious entities with abilities not fully understood, but which seem to pertain to energies such as heat, motion, light, magnetism, and electricity.

## ELEMENTALS
Abilities pertain to the natural elements of wind, fire, water, earth.

## EVANESCERS
Abilities pertain to *evanescing*, or instantaneous distance-travel.

## FERALS
Abilities pertain to heightened senses, augmented strength and agility.

## LURES
Abilities pertain to enchanting voices and siren calls.

## SEERS
Abilities pertain to visions, foretelling, and predictions. May also look into the past.

## SHIFTERS
Abilities pertain to temporary transformation of host-bodies.

## TRANSMUTERS
Abilities pertain to the transformation and manipulation of material substances.

# PROLOGUE

DREAD ODILE—THE WITCH QUEEN, THE NEW GODDESS OF Dulimurian, the Poison of Perrinion—was dying.

Hollis could feel the spirits straining inside the queen's burned and broken body like boiling blood bubbling under the skin. They wanted out, they wanted free of their mortal host. But Odile clung to mortal life with a strength of will terrifying to behold.

She could do nothing more, however. Her body was too ruined.

Sweat rolled down Hollis's face, into her eyes. She couldn't wipe it away. Her hands were fully occupied with supporting the dying woman's legs as she helped Nane carry her down the narrow staircase; she could hear him puff, pant, and curse behind her as they navigated the turns together. The stink of burned flesh and evil magic filled that close space, threatened to overwhelm their senses.

But worse than the stink were the screams, the screeching cries of spirits both mortal and shade in reaction to the pain the witch's host body endured. These relentless sounds of pure spirit brutally assaulted Hollis's shadow senses until more than once she had to pause, lean her shoulder against a wall, and wait for a wave of nausea to pass before she could continue. The temptation was nearly overwhelming to drop her burden right then and there and flee, shrieking in her own utter terror.

But no. Too many of her brothers and sisters had died that day. She would see this through.

At last they reached the bottom of that seemingly endless stair and stepped out into the red remnants of daylight. Above them loomed the massive oblidite idol of

Odile herself, its arm outstretched in benediction above the smoldering remains of her city. Clouds of smoke and foul magic rose from Dulimurian's ruined streets, an incense worthy of its unholy goddess.

"Hollis. Hollis!"

Nane's voice cut through her stupor. She looked back over her shoulder and saw him nod, indicating they should put down their burden. She obliged, and they laid the dying woman on the oblidite paving stones. Odile moaned, her blackened lips moving, trying to form words. A stream of guttural, horrible sounds poured from her throat. Hollis backed away quickly, staring at this ruin of what had once been human.

Odile had always been unnaturally beautiful. In most mortals, prolonged shade possession worked a decaying effect on the body, leaving the host riddled with black bruises, rotted teeth, limp hair, and withered flesh. Not Odile. Somehow, over the long years of her possession, she had only become more beautiful, a creature of awe-inspiring power and glory.

Nothing of that glory remained now. All her long black hair had burned away, leaving behind the melted skin of her scalp. Her head was a festering, bloody mess, and the rest of her body fared little better. She was a mass of bubbling burns, raw, black, and pulpy.

The Crown had done its intended work.

Movement drew Hollis's eye. A red-hooded figure appeared, climbing the wide steps leading up to the platform on which Hollis and Nane stood. It was Venator Hugon, one of the six venators Fendrel had held back from joining the Death Song. His hood was thrown back, and blood, dirt, and tears streaked his black beard. His ascendant shade brimmed with power, and by that power he carried a heavy block in his arms, so massive that no mere mortal would be able to lift it.

Hugon let it crash to the ground before Nane and Hollis, then turned flashing eyes down to Odile's ravaged face. "That's for you, Your Majesty," he said, and spat a glob of blood on the stone. "A pillow to rest your head upon."

Hollis's stomach jolted. She knew what this was. She knew what was about to happen.

The prophecy said that the Chosen King must cut off the Poison's head.

Her hand moved slowly, almost unconsciously, to the quivers of poisons across her breast. It would be wiser—safer—to deal the Gentle Death. A violent beheading would empower the spirits inside Odile's body and send them hurtling out into the ether. The Evanderians would be hard-pressed to catch them and see them properly ousted to the Haunts. Using the Gentle Death would be safer.

But . . . would it fulfill the prophecy? Could they risk thwarting the spoken will of the Goddess?

"*Odile will die tomorrow,*" Fendrel had said to her just last night. "*But it must be the* right *death, or everything we've worked to accomplish will be undone.*"

Now the moment was come. The chopping block lay before her where Venator Hugon had hurled it, and the queen was at their mercy. In mere moments, Fendrel and his brother would descend the idol's winding stair, and Guardin du Glaive would draw his sword, still sharp from the smithy's work the night before, not yet used this day. Then the blow would fall, and . . .

If she was going to deliver the Gentle Death, it had to be now.

Hollis's lungs tightened. She felt Nane's eyes turning toward her, but she couldn't bear to meet her hunt brother's gaze. She forced her hand to relax, to drop back to her side. Empty.

She would see this through.

Footsteps sounded on the stair. Hollis looked back to see moving shadows in the doorway. Fendrel stepped through, turning sideways to get his broad shoulders through the narrow opening. His face was scarred—not with any physical cuts, but with deep spiritual wounds, deep gouges into his soul. He had commanded so many deaths today.

Guardin followed his brother, stepping behind him into the glare of the sinking sun. While Fendrel was haggard, worn, his braided hair coming undone around his ears, his leather jerkin spattered in blood and gore, his body sagging with exhaustion, Guardin's armor gleamed brilliant gold and silver, and his close-cropped hair seemed to glow like a halo around his sharply angled face.

Moving as though on some silent command, Hollis and Nane crouched and caught Odile by her arms, lifting her until she sagged on her knees between them. When

Guardin's gaze fastened on his enemy, Hollis saw a flash of fear in his eyes. She quickly looked away from this disturbing sight.

Fendrel met her gaze. Just for an instant, his eyes locked with hers.

Did he suspect what she had considered doing? She couldn't tell; she couldn't read his face.

His gaze traveled from her to Nane to Hugon, then on to the three other hooded figures approaching through the magic-thickened air. "Hollis and Eloisia," he said. "Nane, Hugon, Rolant, and Wace."

These were the six. The six handpicked by Fendrel not to participate in the day's sacrifice, in the playing of the Death Song. The six who must outlive their brethren to complete a final, terrible task.

The six, along with Fendrel, who would carry the weight of two hundred deaths on their shoulders for the rest of their lives.

At the sound of Fendrel's voice, a spasm shuddered through Dread Odile, right up her spine. Bracing herself in the grasp of her captors, she straightened, and her grotesque head rolled on her sagging neck. Her eyes were scorched, but she tried to peer up at Fendrel. Hollis noted how she spared not a glance for Guardin. She knew who her true enemy was. She knew who had brought about her ruin. It didn't matter who dealt the final blow. Her downfall was of Fendrel's creation.

The Witch Queen's lips moved. A croaking, gasping horror of a voice whispered through her lips, speaking unintelligible words.

Fendrel strode across the gleaming black stones to stand over Odile. Hollis saw an entire lifetime's worth of thoughts whirl through his eyes as he gazed down at her. All the things he wished to say, the accusations, the rage.

But he was Fendrel du Glaive. He never yielded to any emotion, any weakness. In the end, he said only, "Hold her." He motioned harshly to Hollis and Nane. "Hold her still."

With a short nod, Nane glanced Hollis's way. Together they stepped forward, dragging the witch to the stone, and spread her over the block. She sagged against it, dropping her head, stretching out her neck. Every movement was an agony to her seared flesh, and she gasped and choked as tears trickled down her blackened cheeks. Her lips moved again, whispering words Hollis could not hear. Perhaps it was a prayer. But the Goddess certainly would not hear the prayers of such a blasphemous demon.

Fendrel looked round at the small gathering at the feet of the massive oblidite idol. His eyes gleamed with shadow-light and tears. "My friends," he said. "My brothers and sisters, I held you back today for a purpose. Though I know every one of you longed to give your all alongside your brethren, there is one more spell song to be performed. The Word of our Goddess declares that the Chosen King must cut off the head of his enemy."

He indicated Odile with a sweep of his hand. She wheezed a breath and closed her eyes, nestling her head against the chopping block as though it were the softest silk. "The spirits contained within this host will be violently launched. It is up to us to ensure they do not escape. It is up to us to hold tight until the Haunts have opened to claim their dues. The variations of the spell are many and complex. You must work together."

Venatrix Eloisia drew her Detrudos pipes and snapped them into position. Venator Hugon did as well, but

Venators Rolant and Wace both hesitated. Hollis saw in their faces the same arguments she herself had made: *Why are we not dealing the Gentle Death? Why are we risking so much for the sake of words spoken centuries ago by a Goddess we've never seen?*

But neither venator spoke these protests. First Wace, then Rolant pulled forth their pipes and braced themselves. Their shades, called to high ascendancy for this day of battle, flared bright in Hollis's shadow sight.

Fendrel unsheathed his Detrudos as well and gripped it in one hand, at the ready. He nodded to the Evanderians, and they lifted their instruments to their lips and began to weave the spell song, calling forth first the deep drones and then the lilting melodies. Each chose a different variation, and Hollis, watching with shadow sight, saw how the various threads of magic wove together, forming a spell far more profound than any single venator could produce alone.

Lifting his right hand, Fendrel made the sign of blessing, touching his forehead, his heart, his mouth. He spoke then, his mortal voice clear and hard as a diamond, and perfectly woven into the spirit music:

*"A great poison will spread through the Heart of My Children, giving rise to Falsehood reigning in the name of Truth."*

A chill raced up the back of Hollis's neck. The words of the prophecy were as familiar to her as her own name. But to hear them now, in this moment of reckoning . . . it was almost too much. She dug her fingers into Odile's burned arm, afraid to let the moment slip away, afraid that one wrong move on her part would ruin everything.

*"But I will send a champion,"* Fendrel continued, turning his gaze from Odile to his brother standing across from him at the block with one hand on the pommel of his sword. *"I will send the Man whom I have Chosen to cut off the head of the False One and lead my children back to Me."*

With those words, Fendrel took a step back, sweeping his hand in a gesture of readiness. Hollis, scarcely able to breathe, looked up at the Chosen King, as did all the others gathered there, except Odile herself. She stared off into nowhere, her lips still moving in that incomprehensible muttering.

The young king gripped his sword and began to draw it. But he paused and looked to his older brother. As an un-taken, he could not hear the song spell played by those around him. He could not see the power and magic fairly bursting from their souls. His mouth worked, and he licked his dry lips. "If . . . if her spirit is loose, could she not possess me?"

Such words were not what Hollis hoped to hear from the Chosen King at this particular moment. She suppressed a frustrated curse.

Fendrel's face was iron hard. "You are untorn," he said, his voice as firm as ever. "You cannot be taken. No matter what she tries, she cannot touch you. You are the Goddess's own. You are the Chosen King."

Guardin cast a swift glance down at the witch, then away, as though he couldn't bear to look at her for fear of scalding his eyes with the sight. "But, brother—"

In two strides, Fendrel stepped to the king's side and gripped him by the arm. A wild desperation flashed in his eyes, almost too briefly to be seen. Only Hollis, who knew him so well, recognized it. She felt it like a bolt of lightning to her heart.

"You can do this," Fendrel growled. "You *must* do this."

*You must make good the deaths I ordered.*

*You must make good the slaughter I orchestrated.*

*You must make good my faith.*

Hollis heard the words as clearly as though he'd spoken them out loud. Guardin did too. She saw the terror in his face. Terror, not of Odile or the Goddess or the future ahead of him. Terror of Fendrel. Terror of what disappointing Fendrel would mean.

They were in this together. Far, far too deep to retreat now.

The young king nodded. Fendrel stepped back, this time to stand behind Hollis. Guardin drew his sword, which gleamed like a star in the fading sunlight. Its edge was as thin as a blade of glass, as sharp as a razor tooth. It could cut off a finger with a mere touch. That scrawny neck outstretched across the stone should be nothing for this steel.

Guardin took a wide stance beside the chopping block. Hollis forced her vision to focus down on the witch she was holding in place. The monster, the murderess, the enslaver and torturer. The Poison of Perrinion. The false goddess.

Now was the moment. Now, now, *now!*

The king lifted his sword high above his head. A final burst of sunlight penetrated the clouds and the haze of dark magic, flashing against the steel so that it flared red as blood.

Odile's mouth twisted into a smile.

She screamed: "*Cravan druch duima cró!*"

In the same instant, Hollis felt a jolt of pure power, pure horror from behind her, as Fendrel took a lunging step. "NO!" he shouted.

The blade fell.

Flesh and bone separated with a thick thud. The witch's head rolled, and black blood poured out across the stone, across the polished paving stones.

An explosion of shrieking spirits—shade and mortal entwined—burst from the corpse, propelled by that violence and pain, bolting straight up into the spreading song spell woven by the four Evanderians. It struck the spell, a flash of magical force.

As one, Hugon, Eloisia, Rolant, and Wace dropped their pipes, dropped open their jaws, screaming as their own spirits and shades streamed out from their bodies. Their voices broke off in an instant, and they fell dead.

Their spell song shattered into a thousand pieces of nothingness.

# CHAPTER I

## TWENTY YEARS LATER

AYLETH WOKE WITH A GASP.

The world was dark around her. Something heavy weighed her down, crushing her so that she could hardly breathe. Was this a nightmare? No, it had to be the waking world, unless she'd somehow awakened inside another dream. A dream of impenetrable shadows, a dream of burning pain, a dream of constricting tightness and smothering weight.

A dream of . . . itching?

She frowned. Scratchy, prickly itching raged across her body, and she realized that the weight holding her down was a wool blanket. The tightness around her chest was only bandages wrapping her torso.

Slowly, painfully, her mind pulled back into reality. A blurred, fuzzy-edged sort of reality. She couldn't quite distinguish dreams from recent memories. When she closed her eyes, the darkness filled with black bursts of poison, and the bandages weren't bandages anymore but witch's arms holding her tight. She saw a flash of entwined souls, a gouge in the fabric of reality, the opening jaws of the Haunts . . .

A gaping void. Chaos.

She opened her eyes again, pulling herself back into the waking world. It wasn't as dark this time. Either several hours had passed in what felt like a blink, or her vision had simply clarified. Either way, this time when she lifted her eyelids, she gazed up into the shadows of a canopied bed.

"*Laranta?*" she whimpered inside her head.

Her wolf shade moved and possibly answered. But it was all so distant, so hazy, so muffled.

With a growl in her throat, Ayleth recognized the blurriness ensnaring her awareness: *sòm*. Distantly she remembered a tall, blunt-faced venatrix pouring a dose of the opiate down her throat, forcing her to sleep, and, more importantly, forcing her shade deep down into the darker parts of her soul. It was a common practice when treating a wounded Evanderian. Shades liked to take advantage when they found their host bodies in a vulnerable state. But Laranta wasn't like that. Laranta wouldn't hurt her.

She tried to curse but couldn't figure out how to use her mouth. Her lips felt numb and buzzy.

The witch.

Ayleth's breath hitched as the thought plowed suddenly and painfully through her haze, like a monster's horned head suddenly looming through heavy mist. The witch! The Phantomwitch, Inren di Karel! Ayleth fixed her mind on the face flashing so vividly through her memory. That once-beautiful face, with its delicate features and wide eyes, now marred by a hideous growth, emaciated and disgusting.

Was she dead? Or had Ayleth only dreamed she'd

killed her, only imagined the whole battle in her feverish, drugged state? Was the Phantomwitch still out there, still alive . . . and killing people?

By the Goddess's three holy names, was she a venatrix or not? What was she doing, still lying down?

Her heart quickened its already galloping pace. She sat upright in the bed . . . and almost collapsed back on the pillows again. The dim room spun wildly. Closing her eyes, Ayleth hid her face in her hands, waiting for her equilibrium to return.

When at last she could bear to look again, she saw a sliver of light peeking between the drawn bedcurtains. Morning light. But which morning? How long had she lain here unconscious? And . . . and who had found her and put her in this bed?

"*Laranta, where are you?*" She spoke frantically inside her head, but no answer came. Rage without focus welled up in her soul, and the leaden blankets were suddenly unbearable. Summoning up what strength remained to her, Ayleth flung them back.

Haunts damn it, she was practically naked! Clad in nothing but a thin shift, her skinny legs and bare feet exposed. Why did people keep stealing her clothes? She had to get out of there. She had to find trousers. She had to . . .

She collapsed in a heap of arms and legs on the floor the moment she slid out of bed. There she lay, a million pinpricks assaulting her limbs. The *sòm* had numbed her extremities.

Well, it didn't matter. It didn't! She was mistress of her own limbs.

With no regard for her own dignity, Ayleth crawled to the foot of the bed and used the bedpost to haul herself upright. Intense pain sparked up her legs, but she used that pain to channel her rage. Balancing as best she could, she staggered to the door.

It was unlocked. She put her ear to it. No sounds of wailing, no indications of witch-presence. But the witch was out there. She just knew it.

Ayleth hauled the door open, hung heavily on its handle for a moment, then drifted out into the hall. Half dressed, half drugged. Incapable of coherent thought. Her shoulder hit the far wall, and she bounced, staggered a few more paces, and hit a door on the other side of the passage. Her feet dragged, and her mouth gaped. She ricocheted into the wall again, and it took every ounce of will she possessed to keep from sliding down to the floor.

But she was going to kill that witch. Goddess help her.

Ahead of her was the railing overlooking the entrance hall. Vaguely recalling the hostages she'd seen down below—or was that a dream too?—Ayleth stumbled on, moving like a drunken sailor on a stormy sea. Her stomach hit the rail, and she grabbed hold with both hands, leaning way out, her hair cascading on both sides of her face. The distant floor seemed to rise toward her, spinning slowly, and she choked on a gasp.

"Great Goddess!" a high voice exclaimed. "What are you doing?"

Two hands gripped her arms, dragging her back with slight strength but great determination. Ayleth's knees buckled, and she sank toward the floor. Thin arms wrapped around her, keeping her somewhat upright. Finding herself pressed up against a young woman with enormous blue eyes and short-cropped hair, Ayleth gaped and rubbed a finger across the woman's scalp.

"Fuzzzzzzzy," she said. "Fuzzzzy fur."

"Um." The woman blinked several times. "You don't look well, Venatrix. Here, let me help you sit down."

But as the stranger tried to guide her down toward the floor, a bolt of recognition struck Ayleth hard. The witch! This woman, she looked like the witch! Sure, the witch also had a growth covering most of her face, but perhaps she'd . . . lost it somehow?

Ayleth lifted a trembling hand and tried to strike the girl in the face. She missed and hit the wall.

"Careful! Did you hurt yourself?" The girl awkwardly helped Ayleth sit with her shoulder against the wall. Ayleth latched onto her arm, squeezing hard, and when the girl tried to stand, she ended up pulled down onto one knee. "Um," she said, trying to pry Ayleth's fingers loose.

But Ayleth couldn't let go. No. She had to kill this witch. Send her hurtling into the Haunts where she belonged. She tried to speak, but the words caught on her tongue and tangled, and she ended up coughing instead, doubling over.

"There, there," the woman murmured, one hand rubbing circles on Ayleth's back. "There, there. You'll be all right. I'll find someone to help you back to bed. Wait here."

With a firm tug, she pulled herself free and stood. As she tried to take a step, Ayleth caught hold of the edge of her gown, tugging like a small child yanking her mother's hem. "I've got . . . you . . . now!" she rasped.

The girl stared down at her, perplexed, her brows drawing together. "Um," she said.

"Di Ferosa!"

Even in her drug-addled state, Ayleth recognized that voice. Still clinging to the girl's robe, she swung her heavy head around, fixing what she hoped to be a ferocious glare on the approaching figure. He was tall, clad in a venator's uniform, his red hood thrown back across his shoulders. Black curls spilled over a high, dusky forehead, and prominent dark brows drew tight over a pair of piercing ice-cold eyes.

"T'rrr'n," Ayleth said, somehow managing to speak his name with no vowels. "T'rr'rr'rr'n. You . . . ass."

For a moment, Terryn looked as surprised as she felt. They blinked at each other.

Then his expression hardened. He swooped down

over her, his cloak billowing like wings. Only then did Ayleth become vaguely aware of two figures behind him, a man and a woman, both in Evanderian garb. "Let go of Lady Cerine at once," Terryn growled, prying her fingers free.

"Ass." She smiled as the word slipped out more easily than it had the first time. She held up one trembling finger and pressed it against the tip of his long nose, pushing it as far to one side as she could make it go. "You're a—"

"Yes, I'm aware." He smacked her hand away and scooped her up under the arms and knees. "And you're drugged out of your wits."

The world *whooshed* by as he lifted her, and for a moment she thought she'd be sick right down the front of him. While Terryn adjusted his grip, getting his balance, she wrapped her arms around his neck and nuzzled her face just below his ear. Haunts damn him, why did he have to smell so good? Like cedar and lye soap and just a hint of musky horse.

She closed her eyes, breathing deep, then murmured in a whispering sigh, "Ass."

She felt his jaw tighten and his throat constrict in a hard swallow.

"Is she going to be all right?" the young woman spoke from somewhere near Ayleth's shoulder. "She looks so unwell."

A voice Ayleth didn't know responded. "She's none of your concern." She lolled her head about, trying to get a look at the speaker. "Get her to her room."

Ayleth caught a glimpse of hard, iron-gray eyes peering out from under a black hood. Eyes that brimmed with shadow-light. Suddenly, all the weird, blurry, pinprick sensations coursing through her blood seemed to freeze, leaving her numb to everything except . . . not fear, exactly. She couldn't be afraid in this state. It was more of a profound, stomach-clenching sort of unease.

Only as Terryn bore her back to her room and plunked her roughly down on that awful, soft prison of a bed did she begin to recall that the black hood meant something. And only after the two strangers also stepped into the room and the man commanded, "Shut the door," did she realize exactly what it meant.

Venator Dominus Fendrel du Glaive. The Black Hood

of the King.

Ayleth sat bolt upright on the bed, her mouth dropping open. Horror rushed so furiously through every vein that it seemed to purge the *sòm* from her system then and there. Although she still couldn't feel Laranta, though she still felt as if she looked at the world through a blurry veil, she knew what a terrible, unforgivable fool she'd just made of herself. Wandering the halls of Dunloch while practically naked! And whose skirt had she been clinging to? Who was that woman she had just tried, however futilely, to kill?

"It seems she has suffered no lasting physical effects," said a voice Ayleth found vaguely familiar. A woman's voice lacking any womanly quality whatsoever. A tall venatrix approached the bed and placed a heavy hand on Ayleth's shoulder, forcing her back down onto the pillows. "You shouldn't be up yet," she said. "You've had a terrible shock."

"Wh-what happened to me?" Ayleth pushed the words out with her thick tongue.

"You breathed in pure *oblivis*," the venatrix answered, studying her closely with half-lidded eyes. "Do you know what that means?"

Ayleth managed to nod. The venatrix opened her pouch and pulled out an implement for which Ayleth had no name. It unfolded into a stake the length of a man's forearm, and at the end of it was long, sharp needle.

"Hold her steady," the venatrix growled. The next moment, before Ayleth could even attempt to struggle or protest, Terryn's long fingers gripped her by the face and jaw, tipping her head back. She froze at his touch, and the venatrix took the opportunity to plunge the strange device into her neck. Ayleth tried to scream but couldn't. The shock and pain were too much.

It was over in a breath. Both Terryn and the venatrix backed away. Ayleth, muttering slurred curses, pressed both hands over her throat where the needle had punctured. Blood welled up, warm against her palm, and the wound throbbed.

"Well?" The Black Hood's voice spoke from somewhere in the room. Ayleth started to crane her neck to try to see him, but her throat spasmed at the move-ment. She drew a sharp breath, closed her eyes, and held still.

"I'm testing the sample," the venatrix answered.

Ayleth listened to clinks of glass, to the sound of liquid pouring, stirring, shaking. Several long minutes passed, and the room remained frozen in silence other than the noise of the venatrix's work.

At last, the woman said, "The *oblivis* is purged from her system. I'll send the sample on to Breçar for confirmation, but I detect no trace whatsoever. As far as I can discern, she will recover. But she'd best not be moved for a few days at least. Not until we hear from the castra."

A huge sigh slid from Ayleth's lungs. She lowered her hand from her throat, grimacing at the sight of blood, then looked about the room. To her dismay, all three of them were staring hard at her—the venatrix as though she were some curiosity she wished better to study, Terryn as though she were the greatest of all idiots, and the Venator Dominus . . .

He looked at her like a man who was seeing a ghost.

His eyes met hers, locking so hard, so fast, Ayleth felt the jolt in her bones. Worse still, something looked out from behind his pupils. Something not limited to mortal vision, gazing at her in spirit. She felt its power, but with Laranta so deeply suppressed, she couldn't look back. She felt helpless, like a rabbit caught in a snare as the fox paced ever nearer.

She turned her gaze back to Terryn's as the friendliest face of the three. Which wasn't saying much.

Terryn looked away at once, addressing the venatrix. "Is it safe to ask her questions?" If Ayleth didn't know any better, she'd say he *almost* sounded concerned.

"I wouldn't yet," the venatrix answered. "She won't be able to give you complete answers anyway. *Sòm* addles recent memories, and she might never regain full recollection of what happened that day."

"Wh-what day?" Ayleth muttered, but no one bothered to answer.

"We need to know," Terryn persisted. "If Inren gave any indication of how many anchors she left behind—"

"Everyone out."

The Venator Dominus's voice undercut everything, leaving dead silence behind.

Without question or protest, the venatrix offered a salute, gathered her implements from the side table, and stepped to the door. She paused there, holding it open, and nodded for Terryn to join her.

Terryn stood a moment longer on his side of the bed. His eyes flicked from Ayleth to Fendrel and back again. His mouth opened; his jaw worked. What was that expression in his face?

"Out," the Black Hood said again.

Terryn saluted and, with only a last quick glance Ayleth's way, followed the venatrix through the door. It shut behind them.

The room felt suddenly very close, very small.

Silent and still, Dominus du Glaive stood with his head turned away from Ayleth, his eyes focused on the door. But his gaze peered into somewhere else entirely, studying some vision Ayleth could not guess.

Then, slowly, he turned to her.

"All right," he said, "I'm done with these games. Tell me who you are before I pin your heart to the bed."

# CHAPTER 2

IT WASN'T AN IDLE THREAT.

Ayleth couldn't form an answer, though her jaw dropped open. The *sòm* numbed her tongue, and she lay mute and helpless.

The Dominus strode across the room, looming at her bedside like some deathly specter. He threw back his hood, revealing a face like stone with a square-cut, bearded jaw and braided pale hair pulled back tightly from his scalp. Something about him looked . . . *unreal,* somehow. As though he'd stepped out of an illuminated illustration of Saint Evander himself standing proudly above some shade-taken enemy, his pipes raised to his lips and power radiating out from him in lines of ink and gold leafing. It was all too easy to believe this man was the saint reincarnated, returned to the mortal world to administer justice in the name of the Goddess.

"Do you know who I am?" he demanded.

Ayleth nodded. "Fendrel, Venator Dominus du Glaive," she managed to mumble in answer.

"Then you will answer me, girl. Tell me who you are."

His hand moved, and Ayleth saw the flash of his bone knife as he drew it from its sheath. Would he truly kill her? Would he deal her a violent death with no regard for the powerful force he would release into the world? Laranta was no small, shrinking spirit, and if she were propelled through violence and pain, Ayleth didn't doubt her ability to slip past even the dominus's pipes and take possession of a new host.

"I am . . . I am Ayleth, Venatrix di Ferosa," she answered, the words slurring painfully, "lately of Gillan-luòc Outpost in Drauval. I trained under Venatrix di—"

"Under Hollis. Yes, I've heard the story." He leaned in, and Ayleth pressed back into the pillow, feeling small and weak under that gaze. "I've heard that she took you on as apprentice, and I know that you were not sent to her from Breçar. Neither have you been presented to any Perrinion castra."

Ayleth shook her head, and her brain felt sloshy. "I-I was sent from Vielhir. Castra Vielhir. In Campionarre."

He leaned in closer. The only way she could escape meeting his gaze was to close her eyes. But she didn't dare.

"You lie," he hissed, his breath hot on her cheeks. "You're not from Campionarre. If I write to Vielhir, they will bear me out. They will answer that they have no record of you. I know it. I *know* it."

Ayleth blinked, hardly able to draw breath. She wanted to protest, wanted to shout, wanted to scream that she was who she claimed to be. But . . .

In truth, she knew already that everything she had just said was false. She didn't know who she was. She didn't know where she was from. She didn't even know her name. Hollis had told her the story of a young war orphan named Ayleth di Ferosa, who was taken in by Castra Vielhir for indoctrination then sent to Drauval as an apprentice, due to the shortage of indoctrinates in Perrinion. Hollis had shaped a whole history and told her it was her own.

A history of which Ayleth possessed not a single memory.

Dominus Fendrel stared down at her as though trying to read her thoughts. His lips curled slowly back to reveal his teeth. Ayleth saw how dark his gums were, purple and bruised. Almost against her will she looked down at his hands, the one gripping the bone knife, the other holding her by the loose laces on the front of her shift. It was hard to see for certain with the fingers curled so tight . . . but Ayleth believed she glimpsed the dark stain around his nail beds, the spreading shadow beneath his skin, deep down at the bone.

Shadow blight. It came to all venators and venatrices eventually. Even Dominus du Glaive, as strange as that idea may seem.

Still, he was stronger than most men. Even with Laranta suppressed, even with access to her shadow senses cut off, Ayleth could feel the power of his spirit. It emanated from his core in waves of pure energy. But beneath his mortal spirit lurked the spirit of his shade. And it was also strong. Strengthening every day, as Fendrel weakened.

He saw where Ayleth's gaze went. She spied a flicker of white behind his pupils just before his eyes narrowed. Ayleth wondered for a terrible instant if the dominus would make good his threat to pin her heart to the bed. Instead, he let her go, shoving her roughly back as he stepped two paces away.

"You cannot be," he whispered, his voice trembling with some unnamable emotion. Could it be fear? "You cannot be what I think you are. It's *impossible*."

She didn't know what he meant. She didn't know what he thought. She couldn't even speak, so painfully did her heart pound in her throat. Her head throbbed with terror and the effects of the *sòm* drug.

Fendrel sheathed his knife. Opening his pouch, he pulled out a small, corked vial of some silvery liquid. He pulled out the cork, revealing a long, sharp needle, smaller than the one the venatrix had used on her throat, dripping the strange ointment from its tip.

Ayleth wished . . . she wished suddenly for Terryn. It was the strangest sensation, a need she could scarcely acknowledge. But when she opened her mouth and tried to speak, tried to cry out, it was Terryn's name that began forming.

Before she could say anything, Dominus Fendrel acted. He stepped forward quickly, lunged at her where she lay, and pressed her back into the bed, his huge hand splayed across her chest so hard, so heavy, she thought he would crush the breath right out of her. She caught hold of his wrist, caught hold of his forearm, desperate to pry him off.

"Lie still," he snarled. "You cannot be what I think you are. But I must know for certain. Lie still, or you die here and now. Open your eyes!"

With those words, she felt magic catch hold of her. Anathema magic—a curse. It poured out of Fendrel's soul and into her eyes, stinging as it pushed her eyelids wide and held them so she could not blink.

Fendrel plunged the needle into the center of her right eye.

Laranta roared up inside Ayleth's soul, drawn by the ferocity of pain and empowered to force her way through the *sòm* barriers. Her sudden presence exploded in Ayleth's mind, filling her gaze with visions of the spirit world. Ayleth saw Fendrel's shade looming over her, a great white Anathema wraith with no solid form except endless, reaching arms that seemed to reach out of Fendrel himself, digging into her face, digging into her skull, digging, along with that needlepoint, into her eyeball.

Her wolf shade leapt out of her head, launching straight for that pale spirit. But one of its arms smacked Laranta away and sent her sprawling. The wolf tried to get up, but the Anathema shade reached out easily and pushed her down, holding her paralyzed. Ayleth screamed her name in her spirit voice even as her mortal voice gagged and struggled against the pain.

Then Fendrel pulled his strange implement out of her eye and stepped back. Her mortal vision snapped into place. Though she still saw Laranta lying on the floor across the room, she could no longer see the dominus's shade.

She covered her eye with the heel of her hand, pressing down hard against tears. She almost wondered if Fendrel had torn her right eye from its socket. But no, it was still there, throbbing with intense pain. She rolled over and heaved up the contents of her stomach onto the polished stone floor.

The Dominus ignored her. She gazed up at him through sweaty locks of her unbound hair, watching him study the needle point. Then he dropped it back into the vial of silvery liquid, securing the stopper in place.

"I'll send this to the Phasmatrix Domina," he muttered, speaking to himself. "Then we'll see . . . then we'll know . . ." His gaze flashed to Ayleth's face, and he winced as though the very sight of her caused him pain. "You are not possible. You are not . . ."

Ayleth dropped her head, letting it hang loosely over the edge of the bed. She squeezed her right eye tight as blood pounded in her temples. The soul tether attaching her to Laranta quivered with her shade's pain and fear. Ayleth tried to call Laranta to her, but her shade couldn't move.

Fendrel turned away, and suddenly, whatever held

onto Laranta let go. She sprang up, snarling, ready to hurl herself at the dominus. But he, without looking at Ayleth, said, "Call off your shade."

She obeyed at once. "*Down, Laranta,*" she said sharply. She had to repeat herself three times before her wolf shade crouched, quivering with rage and terror and bloodlust.

Fendrel, meanwhile, went about storing his vial back in its pouch, still without looking at her. Only when he had finished did he look her way again. "You aren't her," he said, his voice like a tomb.

Ayleth could only stare, open-mouthed.

His lip curled with disgust. "I'll find the truth," he said at last. "You'll not deceive me."

With those words, he turned and left the room, shutting the door so hard behind him that the bedposts around her rattled. Ayleth lay panting on her pillows, tears streaming down her cheeks.

What had just happened? What had he done to her? And . . . why?

Laranta lifted her head but otherwise did not move. On impulse, Ayleth slipped out of the bed, collapsed to her knees, and half crawled, half dragged herself to her shade. She flung her arms around that dark, wolfish form. Laranta was a being of spirit. She was not present in any mortal sense. But Ayleth perceived her with utmost reality, and when she closed her eyes, she felt her enormous warmth, musky fur, and raw, feral, unnatural power.

She clung to her shade, weeping, and Laranta leaned into her, resting her heavy head upon her shoulder. At last, Ayleth fell asleep there on the floor.

# CHAPTER 3

CERINE STOOD IN THE CENTER OF THE UPPER HALL and watched as Venator Terryn carried the young venatrix to the east wing. Dominus du Glaive followed, and at his heels walked tall, pale Venatrix di Lamaury. Not one of them had a word or look to spare for her, and she was glad.

She wrapped her arms around her middle, shivering despite herself. She could still feel the pressure of the venatrix's fingers on her arm. A strong grip despite whatever drugs they'd used to sedate her. That young woman was, in her way, truly frightening.

Cerine drew a sharp, shuddering breath. She knew the venatrix had saved her life, saved the lives of every man, woman, and child in Dunloch Castle. She had bested the Phantomwitch in battle and killed her, driving her wicked soul and that of her shade into the Haunts.

But she'd failed to save Fayline.

Bowing her head, Cerine turned back toward the castle's north wing, the strap of her satchel gripped tight in one hand. With all she'd packed into it, the bag was heavy on her shoulder. She watched her feet, reminding herself with every step along the passage that the venatrix had done right. At least, right as she best understood it. She was a product of her Order, trained according to the laws of Saint Evander.

When the venatrix saw a shade-taken witch threatening mortals, she'd acted according to her training. She hadn't looked at that disfigured monster and seen a sister. Only an enemy.

How could anyone blame her for that?

Near the end of the passage, Cerine arrived at the door

of the prince's private study and stopped. Tilting her head, she listened for sounds of movement within. Gerard was downstairs, she knew, meeting with her father for one of their endless discussions covering every detail of the upcoming wedding ceremony and the celebratory ball to follow. A meeting Cerine was not expected to attend. Showing up on time and wearing an appropriately grand gown comprised the entirety of her duty. To that end, Liselle had held her captive in her room all morning.

Her stomach clenched at the memory of standing there on a stool while women in frilly caps surrounded her, poking needles here, applying measuring ribbons there, cutting, stitching, and tutting among themselves over the distressing state of her shorn hair. As if any of this truly mattered. As if the stench of funeral incense weren't still sharp in the air.

As if her sister's ashes weren't gathered up only last night and placed in an alabaster jar.

Exactly four years ago, it was Fayline being dressed in white and gold. Four years ago, it was Fayline practicing the ceremonial words to be spoken on Hallow's Night. Fayline who . . .

Cerine choked back tears. No good came of dwelling on what ought to have been if the world were just. The world was what it was. And she had a job to do.

She tried the latch, found it unlocked, and pushed the door open. Her heavy spirit lifted almost at once as she stepped into the quiet book-filled room. The smells of paper, of leather bindings, of ink and parchment filled her with familiarity and comfort. She could almost imagine herself back in the temple scriptorium with Sister Ilda, bowed over her desk and quietly copying holy texts.

The room was cold, but someone had started a fire on the hearth earlier that morning. Cerine unslung her satchel, claimed a poker, and stirred the coals back to life, gradually adding fuel until the room began to warm. Once the logs burned steadily, she swept the wide hearthstone and stood back, satisfied.

Gerard's desk was clear, offering plenty of room to spread out books, quills, trimming knives, and inkpots. Morning light from the east-facing windows would illuminate her work.

Cerine heaved her heavy satchel to the center of the desk and flung back the flap. Carefully she removed its contents, placing each item around her in an orderly arrangement that would inevitably become disorderly as she became more and more engrossed in her work. Still, better to start out well.

Last of all, she pulled out the leather volume filled with pages of Sister Ilda's writing. And some of her own as well. Dangerous writing. More dangerous than any sword.

Cerine opened the book, turning through its densely written pages until she arrived at the first blank space. It was four days now since she'd last looked over her work, since the Phantomwitch attacked Dunloch. There'd been no time even to think about it. But now, more than ever, she needed to revisit those words, both the original Occidian text and this painstaking translation she and Sister Ilda had pieced together.

Evanderians believed that when a shade-taken mortal was killed, if the proper song spells were not performed, the human soul was dragged along with the shade to the Haunts. Such souls were parted forever from the Goddess's Light. Wicked or virtuous, corrupt or innocent . . . it didn't matter. Those souls were damned.

Like Fayline's.

But . . .

Cerine rose from her seat and paced to the book-lined walls, her gaze flicking from title to title. At last she found a volume she had known would be there, the Holy Writ of Saint Evander. She plucked it from the shelf and rested the heavy binding along her forearm as she shuffled through the pages and quickly found what she sought, the *Seion-Ebathe.*

The Prophecy of the Chosen King.

She lugged the tome back to her desk and laid it, open to the right page, just above her own much smaller book. Then, with great care and delicacy, she extracted the fragile copy of the original Occidian text from her satchel. The characters of the ancient dead language were harsh and angular beside the softer, rounder Gaulian script.

She placed her finger on one line of the Occidian text, her lips moving unconsciously in a whisper: "*Dalath-mi'talrythe.*"

Was she mistaken in what she believed she saw there, in what she believed she understood? Her head pounded. Groaning, she lowered it heavily to rest on her palms. She needed sleep. If, somehow, she could guarantee that Liselle and the frilly-capped women had left her room, she would head that way at once, collapse on her bed, and try to claim a few hours of sweet oblivion.

The door latch lifted.

Cerine's head popped up, and her eyes widened as the study door opened. A tall, tawny-haired figure in a rich green doublet stepped into the room, his face downcast, his shoulders slumped. He turned to push the door shut and just stood there with his back to her, the picture of bowed dejection.

Gerard.

She shouldn't be surprised. It was his study, after all. Cerine swallowed hard, her mind scrambling. Was he aware she was in the room? Should she speak? She opened her mouth, but no words would come. How could she explain what she was doing here, seated at his desk? What if he asked about her work?

What could she say?

He turned around suddenly with the heels of his hands pressed into his eyes, still unaware of her presence. His lips were pulled back in a raw grimace, and she saw the cords of his throat tighten.

Suddenly he spoke in a low, harsh, but clear voice: "Great Goddess above, is it my fault? Did I not pray hard enough, long enough? Did I give up hope too soon?"

His head sank, his chin falling to his chest, and his hands hung limp at his sides.

Cerine shuddered where she sat. But she couldn't remain silent. With a quiet rustle of skirts, she stood up behind the desk, her fingertips pressed into its surface to keep herself upright. "Your Highness," she said.

Gerard started at her voice. His face was terribly pale and drawn as he blinked and squinted at her. Where she stood with the light at her back, she must be difficult to identify.

"Cerine," he said at last. "What . . . what are you doing here?"

She looked down at her work, the curling scrolls, the loose sheets of Occidian writing. The volume of Saint Evander's holy writ alongside her own smaller book. Quickly she bowed at the waist, forgetting in that moment that she was not a Siveline nun anymore, but a lady who ought to curtsy to her prince.

"I'm sorry, Your Highness," she murmured. "I . . . I didn't think you would use this room today, and I . . . I needed somewhere to go . . ." The excuse sounded stupid in her ears. She shut her mouth quickly to stop her tongue.

Gerard drew a breath, the corners of his mouth turning up in an attempt at a smile. "Yes, of course. I understand. I don't want to bother you."

Her eyes flashed to meet his, then looked away quickly. "You . . . you never bother me," she whispered, not certain her words were loud enough to be heard.

Gerard hesitated, looking at her intently. When she dared glance at him again, there was a strange expression in his eye.

Cerine ducked her head, staring down at her work without seeing it. In her peripheral vision, she watched Gerard move toward the desk. He motioned with one hand, indicating the pile of scrolls and papers, the books. "Did the Siveline Sisters send work along with their most dedicated scribe?" he asked, a gentle note of teasing in his voice.

Cerine shrugged, though her heart careened painfully

in her breast. "I brought this work with me by my own choice."

Gerard reached out and turned the volume of Saint Evander's work around to read it. She almost reached out to stop him but chose not to at the last. She watched his golden eyes as they read along the lines.

His brow darkened, and he looked up to meet her gaze. "This is the Prophecy of the Chosen King."

She drew a slow breath, hoping to calm her thudding pulse. "I know."

He lifted curious eyes to her face, no doubt wondering why in the world she would pore so intently over a prophecy already brought to completion. At least, if Fendrel du Glaive's interpretation was to be believed.

But everyone believed it. The Chosen King had cut off the head of Dread Odile, the Poison of Perrinion. He had liberated the kingdom, reestablished true worship of the Goddess, and reinstituted the Order of Saint Evander. With his brother, the Black Hood, at his right hand, he orchestrated the systematic hunting down of all witches and shade-taken, and thus purged evil from the land.

Only . . .

"Why?" Gerard asked quietly. "Why are you reading this . . . now?"

Cerine squeezed her fists so tight, her nails cut into her palms. This was the reason she'd come to Dunloch. Not for a wedding. Not to watch her sister die. *This* moment. This moment when she confessed her sins, her heresy.

This moment when she told the Golden Prince what she had found and, in telling him, placed her life in his hands.

She reached out and carefully, deliberately, picked up her own volume, her own translation. She held it out to Gerard, placing it over the top of Saint Evander's writings.

"I . . ." She licked her dry lips and forced herself to continue. "As you know, I have been studying at the Siveline Temple for four years now. Training under Sister Ilda, who is an expert in Occidian dialects. Three years ago—a year after Fayline was taken—we received a treasure: a shipment of Occidian volumes. Holy Writ of the Priestess Queens, which had been smuggled out of Perrinion at the beginning of Dread Odile's reign and hidden in Suuria. They were discovered and returned to our temple. It was my duty to help Sister Ilda copy these volumes, both in the original language and into Gaulian, so that they might be dispersed to other temples and shrine houses throughout the kingdom."

Gerard watched her closely. His gaze never left her face.

"It was while I was working to translate one of these volumes that I came upon a phrase in old Occidian: *dalath-mi'talrythe.*" She dared to look up and meet his eyes. "Do you know what it means?"

He frowned. "It sounds familiar. Is it part of the original Prophecy of the Chosen King?" A rueful chuckle rumbled in his throat, and he looked embarrassed. "They made me memorize it in the original language. I'm told my pronunciation is appalling. But what you said . . . it sounds a bit like what I learned."

Cerine nodded. "I found the same phrase in another book, part of a different text entirely. But as I read it in that new context, I . . . I realized something."

She drew another steadying breath. Her knees shook so hard, she feared she would collapse into her chair. But she had to stand firm, to present her findings with confidence.

"'*Brother with brother*,'" she said. "That is how Evander translated that phrase. '*Brother with brother, one shade-taken and one un-taken*.'" She picked up the old page of Occidian text and pointed to the line of writing in the ancient characters. "But this phrase—*dalath-mi'talrythe*—it doesn't mean 'brother with brother.' It's more complicated than that. It speaks to a sense of unity, two dissimilar things brought together as one, being made as brothers. Not brothers by blood, but . . . brothers who choose one another. Soul kin."

Gerard stared at her. His face had gone suddenly very hard and closed. He still held the book of Evander's Holy Writ in his arms.

"When I saw the difference, I went back to the original text of the prophecy. And I saw more changes. More slight alterations of meaning. This, for instance,"— she pointed to another word on the page—"*Kelthor*. It means *both*."

Her voice trembled with the passion of her words, the old parchment fluttering in her hand. "'*United in brotherhood, both shade-taken and un-taken*.'" She let the words hang in the air between them.

Gerard's lips moved. She could see him forming the words in a voiceless breath, ". . . shade-taken and un-taken . . ."

"It doesn't speak of two mortal brothers," Cerine said. "The *Seion-Ebathe* speaks of kinship between mortals and shades."

Gerard did not speak. The silence was painful, filled only with the snap and crackle of heat in the fireplace.

"Do you see?" Cerine finally pressed. "Do you understand? It means . . ." She couldn't say it, but she could see comprehension dawning in his eyes.

Shades were not utterly abhorrent to the Goddess, abominations in Her sight.

Shades were not damned forever without hope of redemption, lost for all eternity in the chaos and compression and horror of the Haunts.

The Goddess's will was for unity. Kinship. For shade and mortal to stand together. Thus, She had spoken to her first Priestess Queen centuries ago. Thus, She had always intended.

Which meant . . .

Too many things for Cerine to even begin to describe.

As soon as she'd discovered that one small phrase mistranslated, she'd hurried to Sister Ilda and presented her findings. Ilda first swore her to silence and secrecy . . . and then began to reveal her own discoveries, made over the course of many decades. And with the newly recovered Occidian texts, the discoveries came faster, a veritable deluge.

Everywhere they turned, they found them . . . *almost* words and *almost* phrases. The translation always so close, but altered to reinforce Evander's premise that all shades were irredeemable and all shade-taken doomed unless mercifully slain.

And this belief formed the bedrock of the Evanderian Order. The order of shade hunters. Those men and women who took responsibility for the salvation of mortal souls.

Souls that had never belonged to them.

Gerard's face drained of all color. His eyes fixed on Cerine's work, staring at the page of Occidian writing she held out to him. He had been trained in the basics of the Occidian language, but certainly not well enough to understand this ancient dialect. Yet he stared at it fixedly, as though he could somehow will himself to see and understand what Cerine knew.

Gripping her book in one hand, he laid the Holy Writ on his desk and snatched the page from her. "You must never say such things, Cerine," he said, his voice rough in his throat. "You— Never! They'll— My uncle will—"

His uncle, who had built a kingdom out of his own interpretation of a mistranslated prophecy.

Cerine gazed into the eyes of the man known to all as the Golden Prince. The fulfillment of the *Seion Ebathe*. But she saw only Gerard.

"Please," she whispered. "You must know. If Saint Evander is wrong about one thing, he is wrong about a hundred. Including the ultimate fate of shade-taken. I don't believe Fayline is lost. She is dead, yes, but not damned as we have been led to believe. And the shade-taken—"

Gerard's whole body jerked as though struck by a bolt of lightning. "You can't say these things. Cerine, it's dangerous!"

"There are so many dying." She stretched out a hand

but hesitated. Mustering her courage, she rested her fingers on Gerard's arm. "There are so many hunted down, killed, slaughtered as monsters. All because Evander taught—"

He shook her hand away. For a moment he stood in profile to her, breathing hard, her book still clutched in one hand, his finger holding the page. He opened it and read what she had written, her translation of the *Seion-Ebathe.*

*A great poison will spread through the hearts of my people, giving rise to Falsehood reigning in the name of Truth. But I will send a champion. I will send the one whom I have chosen to cut off the head of deceit and lead the people back to Me. United in brotherhood, both shade-taken and un-taken will stand together, establishing a new legacy under My Name.*

His jaw worked. Cerine knew what he saw—all the ways in which the story he had been raised to believe was false. His entire life was made a farce in the space of a few simple words.

The changes were subtle but unmistakable.

He closed the book with a snap, clutching it in both hands so that his knuckles stood out hard and white.

"Cerine d'Aldreda," he said without looking at her, "I command you, as your Golden Prince, to never speak a word of this. Never. Not to me. Not to anyone." Only then did he dare shift his gaze her way. "Do you know what they'll do to you if they find out?"

They would lead her to the block and cut off her head for her heresy. She'd known that all along.

"This is more important than my life," she said quietly. "How many do the Evanderians kill each year? How many men and women? How many *children?* Do you know? Do you know what they do to children born with shades inside them? Do you know the practice?"

His eyes brimmed with horror. She saw that he knew, but she continued relentlessly, forcing him to hear the words out loud. "They burn them, Gerard. They burn them alive. And they call it mercy, because Evander said it was so. Evander, who twisted the words of the Goddess for— Wait. Gerard! What are you doing?"

She darted out from behind the desk, but not fast enough. The prince already stood before the fireplace where the blaze Cerine had stoked to life burned. Before she could catch his arm, before she could even begin to plead with him, he threw her work, Sister Ilda's work, all those years of painstaking labor, into the heart of the flames.

*"No!"*

She fell on her knees before the hearth, hands reaching. Fire licked at her skin, seared her fingers as she scrabbled for the book. Gerard's hands closed around her upper arms. He pulled her back. She kicked, screamed, swore, writhed. But she could do nothing. His powerful grasp restrained her.

"Let it go, Cerine," he growled, his mouth close to her ear. She wept, her body heaving convulsively. She tried to stamp on his foot, to drive her elbow into his gut. "Let it go," he repeated over and over. "Let it go. Let it go."

At last she sagged. All strength seemed to have drained from her body and soul, and she would have fallen had he not held her against his chest. Tears poured down her face as she stared into that blaze, watching the paper curl, blacken, and disintegrate into ash.

It was like watching Fayline die all over again.

# CHAPTER 4

TERRYN STOPPED IN THE PASSAGE OUTSIDE AYLETH'S sickroom and looked back at the firmly shut door. Every instinct told him he should not leave Ayleth alone with the Venator Dominus. But that was foolish. Fendrel wouldn't hurt her. He had no reason to.

But there had been something in his voice, something . . . dark. Something Terryn didn't remember hearing ever before—

"Du Balafre."

He shot a sharp glance sideways. Venatrix Everild stood several doors down the passage, arms folded across her broad chest, waiting for him. Her eyes glinted with impatience.

Terryn pulled himself upright and joined the older venatrix in a few short strides. "Are you quite done pining?" she said with a smirk. When Terryn offered no response beyond a frosty stare, she indicated the door behind him with a lift of her chin. "Who is that girl? Where was she trained?"

"Drauval. Under Hollis di Theldry," Terryn answered abruptly. "Before that, Castra Vielhir."

"She's talented. Talented and tough." Everild's eyebrow rose. "So, she's your competition for the posting at Milisendis, is she?"

Terryn offered no response, not even a nod.

"And here I thought the outpost was being tossed in your lap." The smirk grew into a full-fledged grin. "Does the dominus's special boy actually have to work for something for a change? Goddess bless the girl. What did you say her name was?"

"I didn't," Terryn answered, and before Everild could

slip in another gibe, he added, "We've got work to do," and pushed past her down the passage, making for the central gallery above the hall. "The Phantomwitch is dead, but we don't know how many anchors she left behind."

"Does it matter?" Everild followed in his footsteps like some festering shadow. "Inren is dead and banished. Her little baubles aren't exactly dangerous anymore."

She wasn't wrong. The oblidite anchors used by Inren di Karel existed solely for the purpose of drawing the witch back into this world when she stepped out into the Haunts. Connected by powerful curse threads to these anchors, she could disappear and reappear in the blink of an eye so long as she remained within a mile radius of the anchor itself. Only Inren could make use of their properties, and with the Phantomwitch now banished to the Haunts along with her Evanescer shade, any of her remaining anchors would soon die. Over time they would blacken from curse rot but remain otherwise harmless.

Nevertheless, Terryn growled, "I'm not going to leave dozens of dead and rotting curses scattered about Wodechran. I'm going to find them. All of them."

"How exactly do you plan to do that?"

He paused, glaring back at the venatrix. "We know of at least one activated anchor: the one planted at Cró Ular, the one we surrounded with the barrier spell. It's still active, still out there. We can trace the connecting curse threads from it to others of its kind, even the inactive ones."

"You can do that?" Everild's eyebrows rose, and her disdainful expression momentarily shifted into one of surprised respect. "You can follow a curse thread after the caster is dead?"

He couldn't. At least, he'd never tried, never even dreamed of trying such a thing.

But Ayleth could. He'd seen her do it before. When Nane du Vincent went missing, she'd found one of his old curses and traced it back to the venator's corpse.

Granted, she'd only managed it by allowing her shade far more ascendancy than sanctioned by Evanderian law. She was reckless. Foolish. Dancing on the edge of heresy half the time. But, Haunts damn it, she got the job done.

"I know someone who can," he said, and again turned his back to Everild, hastening toward the private room he'd been given for his stay at Dunloch. "I'll ride out today and find that anchor," he called back over his shoulder to the venatrix. "You stay in case Fendrel needs something when he's . . . when he's through."

With whatever it was he was doing behind that closed door.

Without waiting to hear Everild's response, he ran downstairs and soon entered his bedchamber, slamming the door hard. He stood for a moment with his fists clenched. Nostrils flaring as he drew quivering breaths, he stared at the narrow bed without seeing it. Instead, he saw that curtained bed with dark tangles of hair spread across pale cushions. He saw a drawn, tense face, and black eyes filled with fear.

He saw a slim, naked, womanly body scored with vicious cuts across the chest and down the sternum to the navel.

Terryn ground his teeth. He shouldn't have left her. He should have protested, should have stayed in that room, should have stood his ground. But his training had ingrained in him an instinctive obedience to any order Fendrel du Glaive issued.

What did Fendrel have against Ayleth? Was it simply that she blocked Terryn's path to taking Milisendis Outpost? Terryn knew the Venator Dominus could be a hard, unflinching man when it came to the accomplishing of his will in the kingdom. There was little Fendrel wouldn't do to achieve his ideals.

He wouldn't hurt her, though. He wouldn't. He'd just saved her life, purged the *oblivis* from her body and soul.

But that wasn't the whole story, and Terryn knew it. He'd seen Fendrel's face the night when Ayleth lay helpless, lost in the pain of that decimating poison. He had fully intended to let her die. Knowing he could save her, Fendrel would have walked out of that room and let the *oblivis* do its destructive work. If Gerard hadn't stepped in and commanded him to take action, Ayleth would be dead.

Terryn wiped a hand down his face, conflicting urges tearing him apart. He turned to face his door, half reaching for the latch. But what could he do? Storm back into her room, demand answers from his master, and stand over Ayleth's sickbed like some devoted watchdog? His gut wrenched with the desire to do just that, and he hated himself for this weakness.

She wasn't his to protect. And she never would be.

Something hot stirred inside him, drawn up by the roiling passion in his spirit. Terryn flinched back from the door, looking down at his own chest as though he could see right through the outer, mortal form into his own heart. The stirring intensified, a sharp, writhing jerk that sent pain coursing through . . . not his body, but his soul.

His shade. Taking whatever opportunity it found, whatever weakness it could manipulate for its own gain, his shade was rising.

With a bitter curse, Terryn spun on his heel and strode across the room. His weapons and instruments lay spread across the lid of an old trunk, all polished, primed, and ready for the next hunt. He drew the Vocos pipes from their sheath. He couldn't remember off the top of his head when he'd last strengthened the suppression spells holding his shade in captivity. Ayleth was having too great an influence on him. She made recklessness look . . . tempting. As though it may actually be possible for a mortal and a shade to cohabitate a single body harmoniously, without the bindings and suppressions required by Evander's law.

Terryn knew better. He knew the horror that indwelled him. And he knew what it would do the moment it got free. As it would someday. Inevitably. Someday when his strength failed, someday when his will broke. He could only hope that on that day he would have a friend beside him to deal him the Gentle Death and save his soul from damnation.

But today, at least, he had will enough to do what must be done.

Raising the Vocos to his lips, he called up first the deep, reverberating drone, then the lighter, lyrical melody of the Suppression Song. The music played into realms of perception outside mortal awareness, and he closed his eyes, letting his spirit sink into that spell, letting the mortal world fade around him as he stepped into a realm of soul.

The realm of his own mind.

It stretched before him, dry as a desert, flat and endless everywhere he turned. With the music of the spell song surrounding him, Terryn concentrated his awareness, envisioning a mortal body for himself in this realm of spirit, complete with his uniform, cloak, and hood. The ground beneath his feet shifted. Deep cracks etched the stone, straining with the desire to tear open great gouges in the landscape. Only the spell songs held it together.

As his mouth set in a grim line, Terryn turned to face the one anomaly in that endlessly flat plain under the raw red sky. A mound of rock lay in a heap that wasn't quite shapeless. If seen from the right angle, sharp eyes would discern a distinctly draconian silhouette—the mighty head, the powerful haunches, the enormous wings, all encased in stone.

His mortal body still playing the Vocos pipes, his fingers deftly picking out the complex melody, Terryn's spirit took a step toward the monster. He saw a ripple of movement along the jutting ridge that was the spine. A voice slithered through the air of his awareness, pulsing with heat within his mind.

*What is my name? Do you know my name?*

Terryn stopped short. In the mortal world, his hands hesitated a fraction of an instant before reclaiming the melody. He braced himself, stunned by the sensation that had shot through him so profoundly. He'd heard his shade's insidious whisper many times before. He knew better than to answer. Shades were forces of meaningless destruction and malice; to name them, to claim them as sentient entities, was to give them power. So he'd been taught since the earliest days of his indoctrination.

*What is my name?* the shade whispered, and the song spells shivered. Along the spine ridge, rock broke and fell away in streams of clattering pebbles. *Say my name.*

"*No.*" Terryn's projected image swung both arms out wide. The Song of Suppression rose in a wild frenzy of skirling melody, and in this realm of mind, Terryn summoned up the rock, sending it crawling up and over that misshapen being, burying it in layer upon layer. The shade gave a last screech before its voice was entirely swallowed up.

In the mortal world, Terryn opened his eyes. His suddenly numb and limp fingers dropped the Vocos pipes, and they landed partway under his bed. He didn't immediately stoop to pick them up but stood staring into nothing, his physical eyes still seeing that realm of spirit in flashing images across his mind.

That was too close. He'd almost let the shade break

free . . . all because of a name. All because . . . because in his secret-most heart, he wished he could trust his shade.

The way Ayleth trusted hers.

"Haunts damn," he snarled, and pressed the heels of his hands against his cheekbones, his fingers digging into his forehead and scalp. "Haunts damn that girl!"

His shade was well suppressed now though. A little too much, probably. He might as well be an un-taken. Even his access to shadow sight was temporarily cut off. Ordinarily he wouldn't set out on a hunt this way.

But he didn't anticipate meeting a shade-taken in the ruins of Cró Ular. The Phantomwitch was dead and gone, and other shades would avoid a site of such ruinous old magic. For what he needed to accomplish, he wouldn't require shade power.

The suppression spell weighing like a heavy boulder in the center of his spirit, Terryn strapped on his sheaths, his quivers, his holster and scorpiona. He fetched the Vocos from the floor and sheathed them alongside the Detrudos. Just as he was pulling his red hood over his head and securing it at the shoulders of his jerkin, a frantic pounding erupted on his door. Terryn opened his mouth to call out, but the door opened before he made a sound.

He stood face to face with Gerard. The prince's face was deadly white.

"Terryn, I must speak with you."

"What's wrong, Gerard?" Terryn took a step toward the prince, who entered the room and pulled the door shut, his eyes shifting like those of a hunted man. "What's happened?"

Gerard didn't answer right away. He cast Terryn a quick glance, then looked away. He paced across the room to the small fireplace, staring at its lifeless ashes with such intensity that he might well have brought flames back to life with the heat of his eyes. From there, he moved to the window and stood with his back to Terryn for some moments, staring beyond the greensward and the stone retaining walls to Loch du Nóiv's shining waters.

Terryn watched him with some impatience. "My prince?" he ventured at length.

The prince spun on his heel. "Terryn," he said, his voice harsh and low, "do you ever wonder . . .?"

Terryn waited. Gerard's mouth was open, and his eyes were hard under tightly drawn brows, as though he couldn't bear to say the words on his tongue. "Wonder what?" Terryn pressed.

"Do you ever wonder if what you do is right? Not simply lawful, but truly right?"

Terryn frowned. "What do you—"

"I mean your work. Your duty as a venator."

A heavy block of silence fell between them as Terryn stared into the face of his prince and Gerard stared back, waiting for an answer. Terryn blinked. And in that flash of darkness behind his eyelids, he saw himself in a moonlit forest, his arms wrapped around a trembling child who clutched his neck and wept as he comforted her. Across from him stood Ayleth, her hands clenched into fists, her eyes bright and deadly with pulsing shadow-light.

His own voice echoed in his memory: "*Death is her only hope for salvation.*"

"*Maybe you're right,*" Ayleth answered, her teeth flashing in a ferocious snarl. "*But I won't let you take her.*"

The image passed in an instant, and he was back in his

room at Dunloch. Gerard studied him closely, as though reading the thoughts in his mind. "Well?" he demanded.

But Terryn couldn't answer. He couldn't think what to say.

Gerard shook his head and paced back to the fireplace, leaning one forearm on its carved mantel. "I keep thinking about that inborn child you hunted a month ago," he said, his head bowed, his overlong hair hanging in his eyes. "I can't forget her, Terryn. A little girl, you said. Not yet four years old. By the law of Evander, she must be killed to save her soul. There is no other hope for her." With an effort, he raised his head, meeting Terryn's gaze. His eyes were too bright, gleaming not with tears but with horror. "Do you . . . do you truly believe the Goddess wills for you—for us—to burn children alive?"

Again, Terryn didn't answer. Couldn't answer.

"Because," the prince continued, "if so, what kind of a deity do we serve so blindly? What kind of a being is this we choose to worship?"

"Gerard . . ." Terryn's voice cracked.

"*What would you have done?*" Ayleth's voice appeared in

his memory again. *"If I'd walked away last night. In the forest. If I'd left you with Nilly. Would you have burned her?"*

It was a question he'd asked himself more times than he cared to admit. A question that tormented him. As much as possible, he drove it out of his head, focusing on the tasks that lay before him, never looking behind.

But someday, sooner rather than later, an answer would be required.

He cleared his throat, but his voice still emerged as a rough growl. "The will of Saint Evander is clear."

"But does Saint Evander speak for the Goddess?"

The world seemed to tilt around him. Only it wasn't this world, but the world in his mind—the cracked stone quaking, the suppression spells straining. His heart seemed to be on fire, a fire that sent pulses of heat across a barren spirit sky.

"How many children have you killed?" Gerard asked, taking a step toward Terryn. His expression said he did not want to know the answer, but he pressed the question even so. "How many, Terryn?"

"None." Terryn bowed his head, breathing hard through clenched teeth. "Yet."

The prince reached out to rest his hand on Terryn's shoulder. "What if Evander was . . . wrong?"

Terryn turned away, pulling free of Gerard's grasp, and stepped to the window. His eyes stared out at the shimmering lake. But it was a barren wasteland under a red sky that he saw.

"What if he's wrong?" Gerard continued. "What if the Goddess never spoke to him? What if all that so-called holy writ was never divinely inspired? What if everything we've founded our lives upon is nothing more than a dead man's hatred turned to lies?"

"Why are you saying these things?" Terryn demanded. Though he didn't want to, he forced himself to turn around, to face Gerard again. "You are the Golden Prince. You are the Goddess's gift to mortal-kind. You, of all people, should—"

"Haunts damn it, Terryn, I'm no festering gift!" Gerard flung up his hands, shaking his head vehemently. "I'm nothing. I'm just a man who happened to be born to a man who happened to be made king. And what is my father's claim to any crown? He cut off a witch's head. Nothing more, nothing less. He wore golden armor and looked kingly enough, and people thought 'There's a fine fellow,' and they followed him. While he followed Fendrel, as he's always followed Fendrel. He's nothing, Terryn! He's no hero. Fendrel put the sword in his hand, and he swung it when told. And I? I'm no more than the seed he spawned by bedding a woman who didn't want him, who didn't want me, who only wanted the man she'd been parted from and the son she'd lost—"

"That's not true." Terryn reached out, caught Gerard by the shoulders, and held him fast. "None of what you're saying is true."

"Isn't it?" With a vicious wrench, Gerard pushed Terryn's hands away. "You know it as well as I do. She was forced into that marriage; she was forced into his bed. And I am the result." He cursed bitterly, spitting out the words: "The Golden Prince."

Sickness roiled in Terryn's gut. He bowed his head, his hands returning to the prince's shoulders. His brother's shoulders. He couldn't think of the right words to say, couldn't bear to say nothing at all. He knew the truth of their mother's history as well as Gerard did.

But did that one truth of the past change the truth of

now?

Drawing himself up, Terryn let go and backed away. He adjusted the red hood on his shoulders, adjusted the quivers of poisons across his chest. The heels of his boots *thunked* hollowly on the floorboards as he moved to the door and opened it.

He paused.

"It doesn't matter."

In the following silence, he couldn't bring himself to look around, to meet his brother's gaze again.

Terryn spoke again firmly, his voice clear, hard, and solid as bedrock: "It doesn't matter whether the Goddess chose your father. Or whether She chose you. What matters is what *we* choose. Each of us, each day of our lives. And I choose you, my Golden Prince. Now, until my dying breath, I am your faithful servant."

With those words, he stepped from the room and strode down the passage, leaving Gerard where he stood. He would hear no more of this heresy; he would not shame either of them by listening.

He had a hunt to pursue.

# CHAPTER 5

"VENATRIX. WAKE UP."

A terrible burning stench filled her nostrils. Jerking awake, Ayleth sat upright with a gasp, knocked away the hand holding a bottle of crystallized hartshorn beneath her nose, and snarled, "Get away from me!"

The older venatrix she'd seen earlier took a step back from the bed, corked the bottle, and studied Ayleth closely. "You're needed down below," she said. "Prince's orders. Up."

Ayleth pressed her hands to her face and rubbed hard. Why was she back in bed? The last thing she remembered was falling asleep on the floor, curled up beside Laranta. Someone must have found her, bundled her back into bed . . . and drugged her as well, because she couldn't feel Laranta's presence anymore.

She groaned.

"No one feels sorry for you, girl," the venatrix said, and stripped the blankets right off the bed, leaving Ayleth shivering and exposed. "It's time we got you dressed. Word just arrived that the king's entourage is due at any time. The prince has expressed a wish that you be presented to his father."

"What?" All foggy exhaustion melted away in a sudden flash of terror. She gaped up at the strange venatrix and shook her head. "I'm . . . presented to the . . . *Why?*"

"Because you killed the Phantomwitch. You're the heroine of Dunloch." The venatrix strode across the room and opened the door, ushering in three wide-eyed serving women who were too frightened to look either venatrix in the eye. They carried garments in their arms: trousers, shirt, jerkin, and boots. "Out of bed now, di Ferosa," the venatrix said, motioning to Ayleth impatiently. "We need to get you decent."

"But I can't possibly—"

Her voice broke off abruptly as a melodic blast of heralding horns sounded in the distance. Ayleth looked toward her open window, eyes widening. Then, clutching the thin folds of her shift, she slid out of bed and tottered across the cold floor to peer out her open window. Each step made her cringe, for the cuts across her chest, though healing, still smarted beneath their bandages. She reached the window and gazed across the courtyard, beyond the bridge and the shining waters of Loch du Nóiv, to the fine gardens.

A sickening thrill quivered in her gut. A mighty company progressed along the road, its pennants waving from tall staves.

"The king," she whispered. "The Chosen King."

Others had heard the trumpets. Below in the drive, the household of the prince prepared to greet their approaching monarch. Among them, Ayleth saw the white robes and blue hoods of the Siveline Sisters off to one side, and the elegant velvets of Chancellor Yves billowing from his position on the stairs. The prince himself emerged from the castle entrance, and some tall man Ayleth didn't recognize took up a place beside him. This man was dressed in jewel tones, his vibrant red hair styled tall, lending him extra stature. Beside his peacock finery, Gerard, more humbly clad, looked even nobler to Ayleth's eye.

However, these figures couldn't hold her attention for long; the approaching riders drew her gaze. Straining with eagerness to see the king, she leaned so far out the window, she had to grip its frame to save herself from a nasty fall. The entourage passed under the gate arch and continued across the bridge, banners flying, armor flashing, like a wartime parade. The crowd lining the circular drive curtsied and bowed in a wave.

At the forefront of the procession came a powerful white horse arrayed in crimson and purple, its mane braided, and its head adorned with a gold faceplate. Though an admirer of fine horseflesh, Ayleth spared the beast only a cursory glance. Her attention fixed upon the man riding it.

Guardin du Glaive. The Right Hand of Fate. The man

who ended Dread Odile's hold upon the world and restored true worship of the Goddess throughout the land.

Over the years, Ayleth had gulped down whatever information Hollis could or would offer about this man, this legend. Hollis had served at his side throughout the Witch Wars, fighting to place the crown on his head, fighting to establish the kingdom under his gracious rule. Guardin had been a young man when he faced and defeated Dread Odile.

He was quite unlike his son, Ayleth noted immediately. He wasn't even handsome, not exactly. Not that handsomeness mattered. Whereas Gerard's features were fine, almost delicate, this man looked as though he'd been hewn by force out of ocean bedrock. In this way, the king more closely resembled his brother, the Venator Dominus. However, unlike Fendrel's, his rugged features had been polished to a perfect marble shine. His hair was cropped close to his head and so pale that it was impossible to tell if he had gone gray or not. His eyes squinted into the sun, but even at that distance, Ayleth sensed their piercing glint. Everything about him radiated

95

warmth and power, goodness and strength.

If being in Gerard's proximity could make her knees go weak and her breath catch in her throat, just *seeing* his father made her heart surge with a passion for service, a deep-seated need to cast herself at his feet and swear to him her allegiance. This was a man for whom whole armies would willingly die.

Ayleth felt as though her eyes couldn't get enough of her king. She scarcely had the will to notice the rest of his mighty company, though a small, practical part of her brain did wonder how all these new people were going to fit into Dunloch's already crowded keep.

Gerard descended the porch steps to greet his father just as Guardin drew up his horse at the head of the driveway. Ayleth strained her ears, wondering if she could catch a trace of the words exchanged between prince and king.

But in that moment, the strange venatrix's hand fell on her shoulder. "Come on, girl," she said, speaking sharply. "You can't be presented to the king wearing nothing but bandages."

"I . . . wait. You actually *mean* it?"

"We found no dress uniform among your belongings at Milisendis," the woman continued, dragging Ayleth from the window and into the middle of the room toward the serving women. "You'll have to wear one of mine. It won't fit well, but hold yourself straight and you should manage to be presentable. Does anyone know what to do with all this hair?" she added in a brusque bark.

Ayleth didn't try to protest. When the serving women pulled her shift up over her head, she merely grunted at the agitation to her wounds, and grunted again when they shoved her arms through Everild's dress shirt and jerkin. The garments were all too big, but it was a relief to be in familiar clothing again. The uniform was much finer than anything Ayleth had worn in her entire life, and she felt a little silly when draped with the decorative red sash. Someone tamed her loose hair into a long, tight braid, and Ayleth pulled her red hood up into place, shading her face.

When finished, the serving women backed up, and Everild gave Ayleth a once-over. "That will do," she said and, taking hold of Ayleth's shoulder, marched her out the door.

The front entrance hall had been turned into a temporary throne room, with a mighty chair set before the base of the stairs. There sat the king in all his grandeur, a rich cloak draped around him and over the arms of his chair. Prince Gerard stood to one side, and Fendrel loomed at the king's right hand.

Ayleth paused at the top of the stairs. Her heart froze at the sight of the Venator Dominus. Her encounter with him—was it only a few hours ago?—seemed not quite real. She couldn't believe it had truly happened, tried to convince herself that she must have imagined it in her drugged state.

But one look at the dominus's iron-hard face, and she knew it was all true. And when he turned suddenly to look up at her where she stood, she almost lost the courage to continue.

The venatrix gave her a push between the shoulder blades. Ayleth's knees buckled. She stumbled down the first few steps before catching hold of the railing. The venatrix's hand clamped down on her shoulder. "Go on," the venatrix hissed. "The king is waiting."

Squaring her shoulders and using the handrail for

support, Ayleth descended to the landing with as much dignity as she could muster. But she refused to look Fendrel's way, and she feared to look at the king. Instead, when she reached the landing, she turned her attention to the prince. But his honey-warm eyes were such pools of sadness that she found no strength there. If she continued looking at him even for another instant, she would turn and flee back up those stairs despite anything the venatrix might do to stop her.

Her gaze slid away from the prince, over his shoulder, searching for a tall figure with curly dark hair and eyes like wintry ice. But Terryn was not there.

The venatrix pressed her onward to the base of the stairs, hissing in her ear, "Bow to the king. Don't try to curtsy or you'll disgrace us all."

Ayleth nodded and, without looking directly into the king's face, bowed as deeply as she could. Little spurts of pain shot through her torso, and the bandages felt much too tight. But at least the pain distracted her from the thudding pulse of panic in her ears.

"Rise, Venatrix."

The deep voice belonged to Dominus Fendrel, not the

king, Ayleth realized. She obeyed at once, and as she straightened, her eyes flicked ever so briefly to Guardin's face.

The king looked back at her. Stared with absolute intensity of focus.

A flash of horror crossed his face.

The next instant, the expression was gone. It happened so fast, Ayleth wondered if she'd imagined it.

The world around her went distant, blurry, as though she were once more under the influence of *sòm*. She heard the prince's voice. She heard someone refer to her as "the heroine of the hour." She heard mention of the Phantomwitch. But all these things were too far away.

Ayleth stared at the floor, her heart beating with terror. Terror of something she could not name. Perhaps it was the king. Perhaps it was the dominus. Perhaps it was . . . herself . . . .

"And you will, of course, attend the ball, Venatrix Ayleth."

These words broke through her daze like a rock shattering window glass. Ayleth's head shot upright, and she stared into the prince's strained, smiling face. "What did you say, Your Highness?" she gasped.

"The ball," Gerard said. "The wedding ball on the night of Hallow's Well. Following the ceremony. In light of the services you have rendered to the crown, I would be delighted if you would attend. As my guest, not as a venatrix."

Ayleth stared. Her mouth dropped open, but no words came. No breath either. Her head started to spin, and she was suddenly intensely aware of the king's gaze fixed on the side of her face. She did not dare so much as glance his way.

"Lady Liselle di Matin will see to it that you have a proper gown," Gerard continued. "It would be an honor for both me and Lady Cerine." His eyes sought hers, and he smiled. It wasn't a smile that reached his eyes. "Please do accept, Ayleth."

"I-I—"

"The honor is all hers," the venatrix behind her growled. Strong fingers closed around Ayleth's elbow. "Now, if my king will excuse us, Venatrix di Ferosa is still recovering from her wounds and must return to bed."

Ayleth found herself yanked into another bow, then

yanked again up the stairs. And every step of the way, she was sure she felt the king's eyes on the back of her head.

# CHAPTER 6

EVERY OTHER TIME TERRYN HAD RIDDEN TO THIS SITE OF his childhood enslavement, his soul had felt weighed down with the horror of haunting memories. But not this time. This time, after hours on the lonely roads with a storm of conflicting thoughts and desires plaguing his brain, his spirit lifted as his destination came in sight. At least now he could focus on the work that needed to be done. Anything to escape the wars inside his head.

The sun was already setting. Depending on how long

this next task took, he might have to spend the night on the road. Terryn didn't mind. It would be good to be away from . . . from everything. For a little while.

The binding spell on his shade had weakened enough during his ride for him to switch to shadow vision and gaze down the hillside, to study the ruins of the old watchtower. The barrier spell he, Fendrel, and Everild had erected a few days ago still shimmered, the webbing of their different magics as strong now as it was when they first wove it. Somewhere beyond that barrier spell, somewhere among the ruins of Cró Ular, lay an implanted anchor belonging to the Phantomwitch. They had hoped to lure and trap her here, none of them suspecting that she had already sneaked an anchor into Dunloch, ready to be activated.

It was his fault. Though he tried, Terryn couldn't stop or ignore the guilt flagellating his conscience any time he took a moment to breathe or close his eyes. It was his fault. Gerard had given him the duty of finding the red-haired witch. And he'd failed. He'd tried, he'd failed, and now Venator du Gy and Venator d'Acelet were dead. And Fayline. Poor damned Fayline.

If he had caught the witch first, could he have saved her?

Terryn shook his head. Better not to let his mind wander toward any of these thoughts. Better to focus on duty, as he had been trained to focus all his life. He set his mind on the ruined walls ahead, guiding Fleeta down the hillside. He would find the witch's anchor and bring it back to Dunloch for analysis. When Ayleth recovered, she would help him, and they would use it to hunt down any and all remaining anchors. Together, they would destroy all trace of Inren di Karel from this world.

Dismounting before he reached the shimmering spell barrier, Terryn looped Fleeta's reins up to prevent her from accidentally treading on them and hurting herself. Then, after giving his mare a reassuring pat, he approached the barrier, feeling the powerful hum of magic in his bones.

Something in that hum made him pause, frown. He drew closer, his shadow sight keen, studying that webbing. He drew a short breath.

The spell had been activated. Recently.

Someone—or something—had stepped through and

been trapped.

He took a careful step closer, switching out of shadow sight, and peered across the broken walls with mortal vision instead. With the sun setting so quickly, the ruins were full of strong shadows and glaring light, making it difficult for him to discern anything definite. He moved back to shadow sight, searching for some gleam of soul, something to indicate what he'd caught in his trap.

*Warpwitch.*

The thought entered his head. Or not a thought. A *feeling.* A sense. An instinct of terror.

But no. No, no, that was impossible. He only thought of the Warpwitch because she had held him captive in this place twenty years ago, when he was a small boy. But she was gone now.

"She returned to the Witchwood," Terryn said, though he'd not intended to speak aloud. "She is trapped behind the Great Barrier." He shook his head and swallowed. Then his mouth moved again, speaking against his will. "She returned to the Witchwood. She is trapped behind the Great Barrier. She returned to the Witchwood. She is trapped behind the Great Barrier. She returned to the

Witchwood, she returned to the Witchwood, she returned to the Witchwood . . ."

His hand was in motion, taking hold of his Detrudos pipes. They were out of their sheath, snapped into position, and raised to his lips before he realized what he was doing. The Song of Unbinding spilled out from both pipe heads, channeling his power, winding it into the humming barrier spell.

He broke the barrier with a single twist and watched it unravel in a burst of wild songlike discord that dissipated swiftly to nothing.

Terryn let the pipes fall from his lips. He snapped them together and sheathed them in one fluid motion. Already, his mouth was moving on its own again, speaking the words he wanted to believe. "She returned to the Witchwood. She is trapped behind the Great Barrier . . ."

He stepped to the broken watchtower wall and climbed over the fallen stones. He looked down into the courtyard of Cró Ular.

The Warpwitch stood just below him, smiling and hefting something in her hand.

"Did you come looking for this, my pet?" she said.

She was not as he remembered her in his darkest, deepest, most terrifying memories. She no longer wore the young, beautiful stolen body she'd used when he was her slave. Instead, her host was an angular, haggard farmwoman, her hair lank, her skin cut in a hundred places.

But there could be no mistaking the spirits shining from her mad eyes.

He realized he was still speaking: "She returned to the Witchwood. She is trapped behind the Great Barrier." It didn't matter that he knew it was false. It didn't matter that he saw her standing right in front him. He had no control of his tongue.

His blood turned to ice.

"One of my sister's little baubles," the Warpwitch said, looking down at the item in her hand. It was a diamond, roughly the size of a human eye. Its facets caught the rays of the setting sun, turning it to an orb of fire. "When I escaped that Haunts-cursed forest, I took one of these with me and planted it in a safe place, hoping Inren would realize what I had done and use her extraordinary ability to escape as well. She can slip these little barrier spells of yours, you see, just so long as she has an anchor within range on the other side."

With an effort of will, Terryn wrenched his hand, grabbing for the quivers on his chest. He snatched an Anathema dart, snapped it into his scorpiona, and raised his arm to firing position.

Then he blinked.

And realized he was standing still, his weapon unloaded, his arms at his sides, his mouth repeating the mantra: "She returned to the Witchwood. She is trapped behind the Great Barrier."

The Warpwitch's smile grew. "Was that *your* barrier spell, by the way? I recognized your influence in it. What a handy little venator they've made of you, my pet!" In an instant, like the plunge of nightfall, her smile vanished. "Be silent."

Terryn's mouth shut fast. It was a relief, at first, to no longer feel those false words pouring from his lips. He swallowed, tried to think, tried to sense if he had any mastery of his limbs—

—and collapsed to the ground, writhing in pain. His

limbs flailed, his hands scrabbled, his skin scraped on broken stone. He thrashed for several moments, grunting with an effort to scream in pain.

When the writhing stopped, he lay pinned to the ground, unable to move save for the frantic beating of his heart. He felt the Warpwitch's tentacle-like curse crawling through him, the curse she had implanted in him as a child, the curse Fendrel had supposedly broken. It was still there. Deep down, underneath the puckered skin on his scarred cheek and twining through every vein, down into his spirit.

The Warpwitch approached, tall and stern, her mouth cruelly curved. She knelt and extended one long, large-knuckled finger to press into the center of his burning cheek.

"This is my home," she said. "This is the seat of my power. And yet, when I returned in search of my Crimson Sister, I found myself caught in your spell. So, pardon me if I need to work out a little frustration on you, sweet one."

A scream sliced through Terryn's teeth, and his body spasmed once, violently, as her fingernail dug into his skin.

"I'm guessing you came hunting for Inren. Was this trap set for her? I understand that she took the body of the young princeling's ladylove, but I have not seen her since. Tell me, what do you know of her doings?"

Terryn tried to bite back the words, but it was like trying to force his own blood to stop pumping in his veins. The answer tore out of him in a hoarse, gasping roar. "She's dead. Banished to the Haunts."

The Warpwitch stared at him, unblinking. Then, with a shriek, she leaned in, pressing her nail harder into his cheek until the blood flowed. "You lie. I know you lie! If Inren were dead, her anchors would have broken, but this one I found is still active. She's here in this world even now! Tell me the truth, I command you."

The words came again, and there was nothing he could do to stop them. He told all about the witch's arrival at Dunloch. The hostages. The Evanderian deaths. He told of Fayline, of Ayleth, of Ayleth's failure to separate Fayline's mortal soul and save her from the Haunts. The words poured out in a steady stream, as swift as the blood running down his cheek to drip on the ground.

The Warpwitch listened intently, her lips pulled back to expose her blackened teeth and purple gums. When at last his story ended, she drove her fingernail in deeper. He screamed again, and she withdrew, blood dripping from her finger.

Then, with a wave of her hand, she sent a curse streaking down into Terryn's torn flesh. Responding to her command, his cheek knit back together, leaving nothing but a new, puckering scar, undetectable amid the rest of the ugly scar already marring his face.

"You've done well, darling." She stood and wiped her hand on her bony hip. "You've told me the truth as you know it. I could ask no better of you. Yet." She grinned fiercely. "Forget we've had this conversation. Forget you ever saw me here. Tell your superiors you accomplished what you set out to do. You found the anchor, and it was already ruined. Tell them you destroyed it. Then go about the preparations for your prince's wedding. We never had this conversation."

With that, she pressed her bloody fingers to her lips and blew a kiss his way. "Until we meet again."

He flinched as though a drop of acid rain had landed

on his skin, and when he opened his eyes . . .

Terryn frowned, pushed himself upright, and shook his head. Had he fallen over the broken wall while making his way into the ruins? Clumsy oaf. He must be more tired than he'd thought.

He got up, rubbing his head, which was sore and pounding. Perhaps he'd lost consciousness for a short while. It wasn't like him to be so careless out on the hunt.

For a few moments he looked around, half wondering why he had come to this hateful place. Then, with a shrug, he turned and climbed back over the ruined wall. Without a backward glance, he left Cró Ular behind.

# CHAPTER 7

THERE WAS NO TIME FOR MOURNING. THERE WAS NO time for thinking. There was no time for breathing.

All the guests arriving for the wedding had to be greeted, every foreign prince and dignitary, every peer and knight, not to mention their wives, mothers, sisters, and even several high-ranking mistresses who had somehow contrived to get themselves added to the guest list.

Gerard pressed their hands, offered his knuckles to be kissed, accepted their bows, their thanks, their well-wishes and blessings, all the while feeling as though he were a ghost trapped in this world, going through the motions of life. No longer connected to any of this, to any of these people.

At last, given a spare moment to breathe, he made his way to the west wing and the family apartments, heading for his father's suite. Some small part of his mind perhaps still hoped he could persuade King Guardin to put an end to all this stupidity. Duke d'Aldreda insisted upon the marriage, but not even the duke could gainsay the will of his king. If Gerard could somehow make his father see reason . . .

He approached the door to his father's front room, his hand raised to knock. But there he paused. Voices carried through the wood paneling, low and tense. Then one voice spoke loud enough for each word to be clearly understood: "Tell me my eyes deceived me. Tell me it isn't true!"

Gerard frowned and took a step back from the door. That voice was unmistakably his father's.

"We don't know anything for certain." That deep rumble was Fendrel. "It might be nothing more than—"

"Why have you not killed her already?"

Gerard's heart jumped. He shouldn't be hearing this. He didn't know of whom his father and uncle spoke, and he was quite certain he wasn't meant to know. Yet he couldn't bear to walk away. He stood perfectly still, his ears straining.

"We need to deal with this carefully." Heavy footfalls clunked across the floor. "I will act only according to the law. If she is what I believe, the Council itself will demand her death. No need for any other unpleasantness to come to light."

"By the Goddess!" A creak as though someone had just sunk into a chair. "I thought . . . I thought she'd sprung to life yet again. I . . . I need to see her. I need to see her head under that glass. I need to know that she's still as good as dead."

"No, Guardin," Fendrel answered sharply. "Not now. The door must remain shut, the seals unbroken. We're safe as long as we don't act rashly."

"But that girl . . ."

The king didn't finish, and a long silence followed. No sound, no movement.

Finally, Guardin's voice spoke again. "Has anyone else guessed the truth?"

"Not yet," Fendrel answered. "There are few enough left in Perrinion who could recognize her in any case. Nane would have, but Nane is dead." Another two footfalls. Fendrel's voice was strangely gentle, strangely soothing when he spoke again. "I'll see to everything. I swear it, my brother. But let me do this in my own way. According to Evander's law. In the meantime, I'll see to your safety and the safety of all your guests."

Both voices sank to low murmurs beyond Gerard's hearing. He backed away from the door, treading softly, hardly daring to breathe. As soon as he was far enough away, he turned and bolted, making for his private office. He slipped into that quiet room and heaved a huge sigh of relief. The air was cold. No one had bothered to build a fire on the hearth, but he didn't care. It only mattered that he was alone.

What had he just overheard? He could make no sense of it. Was it possible they were talking about . . . about Ayleth? It didn't feel right. And the rest of it . . . what did it mean?

Head pounding, Gerard staggered to the fireplace, possibly intending to get a fire going. But when he got there, his eyes filled with the sight of a burned book. Cerine's book.

Her book of heresies.

The world around him seemed to close in, dark and dangerous. He backed away from the hearth, making instead for his desk. He all but fell into his chair and sat for what felt like a long time, gazing at nothing, thinking nothing.

Slowly, thoughts crept back in. Memories. Of four years ago, following his first wedding. Following Fayline's possession and disappearance. He'd sat in this same place alone, month after month, unable to form coherent thoughts, unable to feel, unable to properly live. He could only dream vague dreams of vengeance that he knew he would never have opportunity to enact. He had retreated into himself, into his misery and despair, deeper and deeper, until it seemed there would be no escape.

And then the first letter from Cerine arrived.

It was a simple letter. Not long, not eloquent. Written with earnestness and honesty. But in those few pages,

Gerard had discovered his own thoughts and feelings put down in words. Cerine understood. Cerine had loved Fayline too. Cerine, whose mother had been slain that same night. Cerine, who had been sent away to Siveline Temple, cut off from her family and loved ones in her grief. She mourned her losses and, in her loneliness, thought to reach out to the one person who might understand what she felt.

Suddenly, the well of emotion sealed shut in Gerard's soul had overflowed.

The first letter he'd written back to her had been like lancing a boil—gross and horrible, an outpouring of sheer sorrow. He'd made no effort to hide anything. He'd said it all, writing sloppily and angrily, his hand shaking so hard, he'd wondered if the recipient of his letter would even be able to read it.

After sending it, he'd tossed and turned in his bed for weeks, staring up at the ceiling. Wondering if the Goddess would smite him for those things he'd dared put down on paper.

Then Cerine's second letter arrived. In her words he found no judgment, only understanding and truth: firm, faithful, unflinching truth even amid her pain.

He hated her for that. Hated her for what he perceived as simplicity and blindness. He wrote another response and let his anger fuel his words.

But she wrote back again. Still gentle. Still faithful. Still understanding.

He told himself he wouldn't answer this time . . . but within a week, he'd sat down with pen and paper, attempting once more to put his heart into words, curious to know what she would say.

In this way it had begun, a correspondence that passed back and forth until the letters he wrote no longer burned wrathful. Slowly, surely, his anger was purged to be replaced by a simpler sorrow. The sorrow never left, but other feelings began to flourish. Memories surfaced and were shared by both, and more often than not, Cerine's letters brought laughter to Gerard's lips rather than tears to his eyes.

It wasn't until last year, however, that he'd realized the truth: He no longer looked for those letters from Siveline as a connection to Fayline. Rather, he yearned for the connection with the one who wrote those letters.

With Cerine.

No one could have been more surprised than Gerard to recognize what had grown so unexpectedly in his heart. And no sooner did the flower of love begin to bloom than choking vines of guilt threatened to smother it. Of all people in the world, how could he dare to fall in love with Cerine?

But as time went on, he faced the truth: What he felt for Cerine ran much deeper than the fascination and infatuation he'd known for her lively, beautiful, reckless older sister. Cerine was the quiet moon always eclipsed by the brilliant sun that was Fayline. But time had changed so many things, and . . . and . . .

With a terrible groan, Gerard lowered his head into his hands, digging his fingers into his scalp. He'd sent Cerine a letter. Months ago, now. And she'd never responded. After some time, he'd recognized and accepted her silence as a gentle refusal. She did not reciprocate his feelings.

Which made the looming prospect of their contracted marriage the more horrible to him. How could he take as his wife a woman he loved, knowing that she viewed him only as the lover of her sister?

But it was more than that. She'd told him as much yesterday when she held out her book to him, when she showed him her interpretation of the holy text. It wasn't because of her sister that Cerine did not love him. It was because she knew he was a fraud.

The prince looked ahead at his looming future, at his wedding day fast approaching, and he saw only darkness before him.

# CHAPTER 8

EVERILD TOOK BACK HER DRESS UNIFORM BUT WAS AT least convinced to leave behind a pair of trousers. Why everyone was so intent on keeping Ayleth parted from her own clothes, she couldn't guess. Perhaps it was a way to keep her trapped here at Dunloch. Separate a girl from her trousers, and she can't very well go traipsing across the countryside, now can she?

Seated on the edge of the bed, her bare feet just inches from the cold floor, Ayleth grimaced. She'd been ordered to rest again, informed that she must recover properly before the ceremony tomorrow evening. They'd sent her food she could barely eat, then carted it away again, and she realized right around sunset that she was little better than a prisoner.

This thought had motivated her to cross the room and try the latch. Just to make certain she'd not been locked in. It opened easily enough, but there were people everywhere in the passage outside. Fancy people in fancy garments—wedding guests and their staff, bustling hither and thither. She had backed into her room again and shut the door.

Now she sat on her bed, staring dully at a decorative brocade hanging on the wall and feeling the hum of the deep suppression spells wound tight around Laranta.

It was better than being dosed with more *sòm*, she supposed. At least the suppression spells were familiar and didn't put her to sleep. And she understood, of course. She wasn't actively on a hunt, wasn't here on official venatorial duty. She was a guest of the prince, and a guest couldn't very well stay beneath the prince's roof while carrying an ascendant shade.

But she hated it. She hated treating Laranta like the enemy.

Bowing her head, Ayleth pulled at her loose hair, growling softly. What was she doing here? She didn't belong. And she wasn't truly welcome; both Fendrel and the king had made that clear enough. Why they reacted to her with such stark negativity she couldn't guess. But she suspected . . . many things. Many unfathomable things.

Was she really going to sit around for another full night and day just to allow strangers to stuff her into a gown and force her to attend a ball? Really?

"Haunts damn it!" she growled and got to her feet, shuddering at the sharp coldness of the stones against her soles. Darkness had fallen on the world. She could no longer see the embroidered details of the brocade on the wall. The busy sounds outside her door had faded away as many of the noble company retired to their beds following their long travels. Meanwhile, down on the lower floors, the prince's household was in an uproar of activity putting together last-minute preparations for the upcoming ceremony and celebration.

It shouldn't be too difficult to sneak out. To slip to the

stables, find a horse—Chestibor, if she was lucky—and make her escape.

A practical part of her brain reminded her that she had no food, no cloak, and not even any boots. But none of this mattered. In her current fevered frustration, she shook off each mental protest like a layer of fine dust. It wasn't that long of a ride to Milisendis, She could reach the outpost before dawn.

Determined to ignore the icy pain in her cold feet, Ayleth crossed the room to her door once more. Her heart thudded with sudden fear that maybe someone had come along in the hours since she last checked and locked her in. But the latch gave at her touch, and she breathed a huge sigh.

The breath caught in her throat the next instant as the sound of heavy boots thudded at the end of the passage. She peered out of her room, struggling to see in the dark with her limited mortal vision. A figure moved into her view carrying a tapered candle in one hand, its little glow of flame not bright enough to illuminate a face. She could discern nothing more than a tall, broad, manly form.

The sound of boots continued, and a second figure

joined the first.

"Dominus," a deep voice murmured.

Terryn. Ayleth's heart hitched.

When the other man spoke, Ayleth recognized Fendrel's voice at once. "Glad to see you back, Venator du Balafre. I trust your reconnaissance to Cró Ular was useful?"

"I found one of Inren's anchors, yes. It was broken. I disposed of it."

"Good man." The candle flame shifted slightly, and now Ayleth could see Fendrel's hard face, the glint of his eye. "As you no doubt observed, the king's company has arrived. I need you now to set up a barrier spell around Dunloch. Though Inren is dead and gone, and we have no reason to suspect further attack, we will take no chances. Not this time."

A short silence followed. No doubt both were remembering four years ago, the carnage of the prince's wedding. Ayleth shuddered. They definitely shouldn't take chances.

But she needed to get out of here quickly, before the barrier was raised. And those two were standing directly in her way.

It looked as though she'd be climbing out her window again, Goddess help her!

She took a step back into her room, beginning to draw the door shut behind her.

"About the venatrix."

Ayleth paused. That was Fendrel's voice again. Did he mean her?

"What about her?" Terryn answered.

"I want you to keep an eye on her."

No answer.

"Everild is under orders to keep her in her room throughout the day tomorrow. But Gerard has taken it into his head that he wants 'the heroine' to attend the ball that night." Annoyance laced Fendrel's voice. "You will serve as her escort. Don't let her out of your sight."

Another long silence.

Then Terryn's voice, tight and abrupt: "Why?"

"Because your Dominus commands it."

Ayleth's heart pounded in her throat. She realized she'd been holding her breath and slowly let it out through her clenched teeth. Moving with extreme care, she eased her door a little further open and peered down the passage once more. Fendrel had shifted the candle again, and now she could just discern the outline of Terryn's profile. No expression, merely the contours of his nose and jaw, a highlight on one sharp cheekbone.

She saw his mouth open, but a moment passed before he spoke again. "Who *is* she, Fendrel? What is she to you?"

"She's your competition," Fendrel answered, his lip curling. "She's the girl who just impressed the Golden Prince so much that he has bucked all protocols and invited her to attend his wedding. She is the girl who stands in the way of everything you and I have worked to accomplish. Do you honestly believe Gerard will think twice about giving Milisendis to that little chit now that she has styled herself into some sort of heroine?"

"Styled herself?" Terryn shook his head. "She killed Inren di Karel. While drugged and wounded, and without the aid of an ascendant shade. Would that all of us could boast such style!"

Despite herself, Ayleth's mouth curved. A month ago, she never would have believed she'd hear such words from Terryn du Balafre's lips. Warmth pooled in her chest, and she had to take a gasp of cold air to drive it out again.

Candlelight moved and danced, reflected in the darkness of Fendrel's eyes. He took a step closer, looking down on Terryn by several inches. His teeth gleamed when he spoke. "Watch her, boy. Don't let your head be turned. Watch her like you would your closest enemy. And if she does anything, *anything* unfit for a venatrix of Saint Evander, report it back to me at once. Have I made myself clear?"

"Yes, Dominus," Terryn said and saluted.

"Good." Fendrel drew back again. "Now, go establish the barrier."

Ayleth didn't wait to see if any further words were exchanged. She stepped back into her room and carefully, quietly pulled the door shut. The clunk of the latch sounded loud in her ears, and she stood for several heart-stopping moments, straining for the sound of heavy feet approaching outside. None came, however. Fendrel was not on his way to pay her a visit.

Was all of this really just about the competition?

Fendrel's threatening words and looks, the strange and horrible test he'd performed on her eye . . . the king's expression of utter shock at the sight of her . . . was it all simply because she had stepped in where she wasn't meant to be, catching the prince's attention and unceremoniously nudging Terryn off his path to glory?

Somehow, she didn't think so.

Her feet felt like blocks of ice, and she stamped hard, trying to warm them. If Terryn left at once to weave the barrier spell, he could have the whole of Dunloch encircled within two hours. But there was still time enough to get a horse and get out, provided she didn't run into any obstacles. First, she needed to get out of this room, and now that she knew Fendrel was prowling the halls of Dunloch, she didn't like to risk bumping into him.

"Hullo again, window," she muttered ruefully, crossing the room. She pushed open the lead-lined glass and gazed down to the white pebbles of the drive far below.

Had she really climbed down all that way while under the influence of *sòm*? It was a miracle she'd not broken her neck. Yet here she was again.

With a string of muttered curses, Ayleth climbed onto the sill and swung one leg over. Her toes felt for cracks in the wall. Moonlight glowed through trailing clouds, which helped somewhat, but she wished again, fervently, for Laranta's ascendance inside her. She would much rather not do something like this alone.

Just before heaving herself fully out the window and committing to the climb, she paused. As though in echo, she heard Fendrel's words again: *"Do you honestly believe Gerard will think twice about giving Milisendis to that little chit?"*

She'd known from the beginning that her rivalry with Terryn was hopeless. She didn't have his training; she lacked his connections. And she certainly didn't have the advantage of being half-brother to the prince. She'd thrown herself into the competition with all the will she possessed, but not because she truly believed she had a shot at taking Milisendis for herself. In her heart of hearts, she'd always known Gerard would choose Terryn.

But . . . maybe the conclusion wasn't forgone after all? She had killed the witch. She had saved Dunloch. So maybe . . .

"Don't be downright stupid," Ayleth hissed. Her

hands gripped the windowsill until her knuckles turned white. "You killed Fayline. You killed his true love. And you let her soul be dragged to the Haunts. The prince can barely *look* at you. He's not giving you any posting anytime soon."

Adjusting the set of Everild's ill-fitting trousers around her waist, she climbed over the sill and began the perilous descent. Her fingers and toes were numb, but she shoved them into cracks and somehow contrived to distribute her weight in such a way that she stayed flat against the wall. A few handy moldings and protrusions presented themselves as she went, and she managed to reach the ground without breaking anything. She had to lean against the wall, push the loose hair out of her face, and simply breathe for several moments after.

The first of her several difficult tasks had been accomplished: She was out of her room.

Now to get her horse . . . who was stabled on the far side of the island. She could hardly march across the main drive and hope to escape notice, which meant she had to circle behind the huge keep.

Keeping to the shadows, Ayleth crept through arched

access tunnels and along walls, carefully skirting doors and ducking beneath windows, and avoiding such pitfalls as drainage ditches, a compost heap, and the busy torchlit kitchen yard. By the time she reached the side of the island where the stables were located, her feet hurt nearly as much as the rapidly healing cuts on her torso.

Once through the delivery tunnel, she ducked into an alcove in the castle wall to plan her next move. Sentries on the battlements high above were unlikely to pay her any heed, and no guards patrolled this close to the keep, though she knew there were plenty standing watch at the gate. How she would get past them, Ayleth wasn't certain. But she shrugged that thought away. Gate guards or no gate guards, she'd have an easier time escaping Dunloch before the barrier was raised.

Ayleth darted across an open area to the side of a windowless stone outbuilding, most likely a granary. Spying movement on the circle drive, she ducked into the building's lee, crept around behind it, and finally caught sight of the stables. A rather long open space lay between her and the nearest stable door, and at that inopportune moment, the moon burst out from behind the clouds, beaming bright on the gravel pathways and slate rooftops. Ayleth sucked in her lips, dreading the increased risk of being seen while crossing under that light. But she had so little time . . .

She took a step out from the shadows.

A hand caught her hard by the arm and yanked her back.

She drew a sharp breath, prepared to yell, but the air burst out of her lungs as she was pressed suddenly and hard into the granary door, deep in the shadows of its doorway. Someone loomed over her, still clutching her arm with one hand, the other hand clamped over her mouth. Ayleth twisted, squirmed, tried to work her jaw free, to bite.

"Hush," Terryn's voice growled softly in her ear. "Hush, or she'll find you."

# CHAPTER 9

AYLETH WAS SO STARTLED, SHE FROZE IN PLACE. HER mortal eyes strained in the darkness to discern the features of the face so close above her own, unable to believe it was truly Terryn's voice she had just heard.

Before she could make her mind fully grasp the situation, another sound caught her ears: spurs rattling on stones, crossing the yard from the stables. She twisted against the grasp on her arm and the hand over her mouth to see over her captor's shoulder.

Striding through the moonlight came Venatrix Everild. She must have just returned from some errand on behalf of her Dominus, some last task that needed seeing to before the barrier spell was raised. If Ayleth had taken even two more steps into the stable yard, she would have ended up directly in Everild's line of sight, her escape thwarted before it began.

Not that her current situation was any better.

Everild continued past the granary without a second glance. Her shade must be deeply suppressed, otherwise her shadow vision would certainly have spied the two souls pressed close together in the darkness of the doorway. She followed nearly the same route Ayleth had just used, headed for the tunnel leading to the back of the keep. The echo of her spurs soon faded behind her.

Ayleth let out a breath against the palm over her mouth and glanced at the face above her, still unable to discern more than shadows. But it was Terryn, she was sure of it. Now that her heart had calmed its frantic beating, she recognized the smell of him, that fresh smell of the forest, so out of place among the stone buildings of Dunloch.

She was suddenly aware of how close he was, of how he leaned into her, pressing her into the granary door. His breath was warm on her cheek, his lips hovering close to her ear.

When she shook her head, he let his hand slip from her mouth. "She's gone now," Ayleth muttered. "Um. Thank you." She shifted against the door, expecting him to let go and back away.

Instead, the hand he'd pressed to her mouth moved to rest on her shoulder, close to her neck. It felt warm against her cold skin, and she realized that her loose undershirt had pulled far to one side during their short tussle, exposing her shoulder to the sharp autumn air.

"If you are making your escape, di Ferosa," Terryn's unmistakable deep-as-night voice rumbled, "one might advise you to take a cloak. It's a chilly night."

"One could stuff one's advice back down one's own throat," Ayleth growled, flashing a glare he probably could not see. "No one thought to leave me a cloak. No cloak, no jerkin . . . Haunts, I had to borrow Venatrix di Lamaury's trousers!"

"So, you decided to make your daring getaway wearing

next to nothing? But then, you go into battle against witches while wearing even less, so I shouldn't be surprised."

"Who says I'm making a daring getaway?"

"I should think that goes without saying."

"I'm simply checking on my horse." Ayleth let the lie slide right off her tongue, confident it wouldn't be believed in any case. "I want to be sure Chestibor's being properly cared for. You never can tell with these fancy stable boys and their fancy uniforms. They don't look like they know hoof from hock." She tried to shift position again, to edge away and put a little more distance between them. His hand on her shoulder relaxed its grasp, and for a moment she thought she'd slip past him.

The next moment, however, his other hand slid around her waist, pulling her closer than before, and the hand on her shoulder moved to the back of her neck, its fingers tangling in her hair. Her skin flushed, and a thousand prickles of sensation raced up and down her spine. Why had her legs suddenly gone so weak? Was there still some residual *sòm* in her system?

His face turned and, despite the shadows, even though

she could not see his features, she was suddenly, painfully aware of how near his lips were. Lips the shape of which she remembered quite well. Lips she had, not once but twice, pressed hers against, subtle and sensuous and alluringly responsive to her touch.

Haunts damn, what was she thinking?

A growl reverberated in her throat. She wrenched her hands up, grabbed hold of the front of his jerkin and, pivoting her weight abruptly, turned him completely around, out of the doorway, and shoved his back against the granary's stone wall. From this new angle she could see his face, fully illuminated by moonlight. His eyes widened. His hand did not leave her waist but continued to hold her close, close enough for her to feel the coolness of his belt buckle through the thin linen of her shirt. His other hand slid down her neck to press between her shoulders, fingers splayed and firm.

"If you run away now, di Ferosa, you'll make yourself look guilty," he said, his voice thick.

"Guilty of what?" she snapped back, refusing to let her gaze stray from his eyes down to his mouth. "I haven't done anything. Only killed the witch you failed to bring down."

His teeth flashed in a grimace, and the muscles of his arms tensed around her. "If you're not guilty, why did you sneak out through your window in the middle of the night?"

Ayleth's mind spun frantically for some excuse, any excuse. How could she begin to explain her interaction with Fendrel? Or that strange look she'd seen flash through the king's eyes when she was presented? It didn't make sense, none of it did. But she had to say something.

"They're threatening to put me in a gown," she growled. "I'm supposed to attend the wedding ceremony tomorrow night. And the ball, Goddess help me! I'm not a ball sort of girl, in case you haven't noticed."

His grimace tilted into a smile. "I've noticed. You'd look ridiculous in a ballgown."

She was grateful for the silvery moonlight to disguise the sudden flush in her cheeks. The last thing she needed was for him to see that his comment affected her. With an effort, she made her cold fingers release their grip on the front of his jerkin, flattened her hands against his chest, and pushed. It wasn't a particularly vigorous push, yet she still almost got away.

Terryn's face hardened. He stood up straighter, stepping away from the wall she had pinned him against. The hand around her waist pressed against the small of her back while his other hand crept up into her hair once more, cupping the back of her head. She leaned back, reacting on the impulse of instinct rather than conscious will, and gazed up into those ice-cold eyes of his, which were suddenly burning in the moonlight, their dark centers ringed in blue fire.

"Careful, di Ferosa," he murmured, his voice an octave deeper than before. "Choose your next move wisely."

If Laranta were ascendant, she could easily have snatched him up, thrown him over her shoulder, and smashed him into the ground. Even without Laranta, she could probably break this hold of his if she really tried. And he knew it.

Which meant he also knew she wasn't resisting him.

He drew a fraction closer, and the air between them, though it had been cold only moments ago, was suddenly hot.

But Ayleth turned her head slightly to one side, breaking their shared gaze for a breath, just long enough to gather her senses. Then she turned back to him, her face split with a swift, ferocious smile. One of her hands slid up his chest, and its fingers wrapped around his throat. She watched the dark of his eyes dilate, nearly obscuring the blue.

"You want to talk about guilt, du Balafre?" she purred. Her fingers tightened, and her smile turned to stone. "I know that you lied to me. That you lied to all of them: Fendrel, the king, and even Gerard."

"Lied?" His gaze flashed to meet her eyes. "What do you mean? How have I lied to Gerard?"

She drew another calming breath, nostrils flaring. Now she'd begun her attack, she couldn't back down.

"He trusted you to hunt the Phantomwitch. You were on her trail for weeks, all the while insisting you'd found nothing. But I know better. I discovered your secret: I know about the anchor you kept stashed away in your room at Milisendis. I went to Cró Ular, and I saw where it had been recently activated. You were aware all along that Inren was in the borough. And because you lied, good people—good venators—are dead."

Terryn's arms dropped away, his fingers untangling from her hair. He caught the hand holding his throat and wrenched it away. Her training took over, and she tilted her arm hard, attempting to break free, and with her other hand lashed out to strike his face.

But his training had been similar to hers, and, unlike her, he wasn't still suffering the aftereffects of *oblivis* purging. With a well-timed twist, he caught her wrist, whirled her around, and pinned her, none too gently, face first against the wall.

She pounded the stones with her free hand, then pushed herself back up, fight surging in her veins. He pulled a little harder on her wrist, just enough that it hurt, and she went still.

"I don't know what you're talking about," he said, his voice dark behind her. "I have never lied to the prince. I have never lied to Fendrel. I admit I failed when it came to the Phantomwitch, but had I discovered anything that could have made me believe she'd escaped the Witchwood, I would have pursued the lead to its end."

"More lies!" Ayleth hissed.

His breath came hard and fast. "I'm not the liar here, Venatrix di Ferosa. I am not the one with the secrets. I have always been and always will be a loyal servant of Saint Evander."

He sounded so sincere. Sincere enough that, despite her current position, despite the heat flaring through her veins, she wanted to believe him. She wanted to turn around, look him in the eye, and see truth shining in his gaze.

Maybe there was some mistake. Maybe the anchor she'd found had been planted by someone else. Kephan, perhaps, under the thrall of the Warpwitch, before he left for healing at the castra. Or even the Phantomwitch herself.

Sensing her hesitation, Terryn loosened his hold on her and stepped back. Whirling to face him, teeth bared, she took a wide stance, fists clenched, but then she saw the look on his face. Confusion. Frustration. And was that . . . fear? She hesitated, her lip curled in a snarl.

"All right," she said. "Let's say you're being honest." She tossed her head, brushing back strands of hair that had fallen over her face. "How do you explain the anchor

I found in your room?"

"What anchor? You mean the broken anchor we discovered among your belongings after you'd been *oblivis* poisoned?"

That's right. She'd had it on her during her first encounter with the Phantomwitch.

She nodded slowly. "Yes. Yes, that one."

"We assumed you'd picked it up just before your fight with Inren. Somewhere in Cró Ular. Are you telling me you found it elsewhere?"

"I found it in your bedroom. I followed the stink of broken curses to the bottom of your chest where it was hidden in a satchel."

Terryn shook his head. His jaw twisted, and the muscle of his scarred cheek tensed. "That's not possible. I never saw one of Inren's anchors. That is . . . I found one at Cró Ular earlier this evening, but it was already broken and . . . and . . ." The muscle in his cheek jumped, and he drew a sharp breath and turned his head as though experiencing a flash of pain. He pressed one hand to the side of his face, covering the scar.

Ayleth blinked, trying to switch to shadow vision, to

look at him in spirit and see what her mortal eyes could not perceive. But Laranta was still suppressed and unable to provide her sight.

Terryn mastered himself and stood upright again. He pushed a dark curl off his forehead, then turned his head, cracking his neck, and stood up straighter than before, towering over Ayleth. "I have no reason to lie to my prince," he said. "You, however . . . You are nothing but mystery compounded upon mystery."

How could she deny it? She didn't know how many of the things she'd told Terryn about herself were lies. She didn't know which parts of her history were true and which were Hollis's invention.

She didn't know why Fendrel looked at her the way he did.

None of this changed what she had found. Still, it was possible . . . it was just *possible* that the oblidite anchor had been a plant. Inren carried an Evanescer, after all. She could have infiltrated Milisendis and stowed her anchor away there for reasons no one would ever discover. She could have known Terryn was close on her trail, could have done it to throw him off somehow. It was *possible*.

Why did she want to believe such a foolish story? Why did she *want* so much for Terryn to be innocent of these accusations she'd just hurled in his face?

She pulled her shirt straight, adjusting the loose folds over her bare shoulder. Her skin felt frozen once more, and she shivered hard. Her feet were blocks of ice.

"I think we're done here, du Balafre," she said, and turned toward the stables. She'd wasted enough time already.

"Don't go."

She stopped. Her pulse quickened, thrumming in her ears.

"Don't leave Dunloch. Not tonight. Stay at least through the ceremony tomorrow. For Gerard's sake if not for your own."

Sickness churned in Ayleth's stomach. She longed for the open road before her and the sky spreading wide above her. She longed for nothing so much as the wild forested slopes of Drauval Borough, the sheer heights and stone peaks of the Skada Mountains.

Why had she been so stupidly impulsive? Why had she disobeyed Hollis and run away? At the time, she'd believed she needed answers like she needed her next breath. But she didn't even know the right questions to ask.

Gerard's face flashed across her mind's eye, Gerard as she had last seen him in the entrance hall, standing beside his father. He'd not looked like a man on the eve of his wedding. His face was gray, his eyes sunken.

And still, he was nothing if not the proud and noble hero.

Ayleth drew a careful breath into her lungs and held it. Was anyone here at Dunloch worthy of Gerard's trust? He trusted Terryn, but Terryn was a liar. He trusted Fendrel, but Fendrel was caught up in his own twisted agendas. And the Chosen King? He was under Fendrel's thumb. Who remained to stand by the prince? Who would protect him not only from witches, but also from his closest comrades and advisors?

Ayleth di Ferosa. That's who.

She let out a long stream of white vapor like curling smoke from her gut. As she watched it coil and evaporate, resolve firmed in her heart. She may not be the most devout venatrix to take the vows of service. She may not wholly trust the teachings of the saint; she might struggle under the yoke of Evanderian law. But she was loyal to the Golden Prince.

"Very well, du Balafre," she whispered, her back still to Terryn. He probably couldn't even hear her speak. She turned on her heel to look him straight in the eye. "You win."

With those words she stalked past him, passing so close she felt the heat of his body. His hand moved, reaching out, just brushing against her fingertips, and she wondered for a stomach-thrilling instant if he would catch hold of her again, if he'd stop her, if he'd . . . she didn't know what.

But his fingers merely touched hers, the barest instant of contact. Then she was past him, striding back the way she had come, around the granary, making for the great stone keep. Even after she'd entered the passage under the west wing and was well beyond his sight, she thought she felt the heat of his eyes on the back of her head. In the deep shadow, she paused to lean her back against the cold stone wall and pressed a hand against her heart, which beat too quickly for comfort. Her skin still burned with his touch.

Grinding her teeth, she hurried on into the kitchen yard, forcing her cold feet faster. The east wing of Dunloch waited, her lonely window casement open. But now she didn't need to climb the wall again. Now that she was no longer trying to escape, she could walk through the castle's halls and up the stairs with no fear of detection.

Nevertheless, she used one of the kitchen entrances to avoid the risk of bumping into Fendrel on her way. The kitchens were still alive with preparations for the wedding feast, and no one spared her so much as a glance as she scuttled through the chaos. Her skin prickled at the sweat-inducing heat of the many glowing fires, and she was tempted to linger for a while.

Still, the need for quiet, the need for peace drove her on. She stepped into the cold hallway beyond the kitchens, dodging servants as they came and went, and made her way out at last to the stillness of the main keep, beyond reach of the kitchen noise. Flitting like a phantom, she progressed by sense rather than certainty through the labyrinthine halls and passages, searching for a staircase to the upper levels.

A gleam of light caught her eye.

She paused, turning to look down a wide passage that seemed vaguely familiar. Had she come this way before? Something about it sparked a memory, though she had been to Dunloch only a handful of times in the busy weeks since her first momentous visit. These tall pillars and that door . . . Did they lead to the gallery of portraits?

A flicker of candlelight moved beyond that door.

Suddenly curious, Ayleth padded silently across the polished floor, slipped to the doorway, and peered in. A figure moved down the center of the gallery, carrying a candle. A tall, broad-shouldered figure. Fendrel? What was he doing here?

Then the face turned. She saw the profile, not of the Venator Dominus, but of the Chosen King.

Her breath caught. Which was silly, she told herself. Why should it seem strange to her to see Guardin du Glaive wandering the halls of his son's home in the middle of the night? If the king had awakened in the night only to be taken by a sudden urge to gaze on the artistically rendered faces of heroes and saints and priestess-queens of old, why should he not do so? It was no business of hers.

She ought to turn away, to continue in search of her room . . . but she couldn't tear her gaze from that dark silhouette as it continued to the far end of the hall. The king lifted his candle, and its glow illuminated the last of the portraits, hung at the far end of the gallery where it would be protected from too much sunlight fading its colors.

It was the portrait of Queen Leurona. Ayleth had seen it her first day at the castle while wandering lost in the passages. She had recognized that beautiful face even then—recognized it because it was so like another face she knew. The image of the queen held the infant Golden Prince in her lap. The artist had composed her to look like a saint, complete with a golden aura like a halo behind her head, and the baby held its chubby hands up in a holy gesture quite unrealistic for its depicted age.

Leurona gazed down from her gilded frame, staring into the face of her husband with a pair of ice-cold eyes. Eyes so very like those that had, only a few moments ago, burned with nameless passions mere inches from Ayleth's own.

For some time, the king stood still, regarding this image. Perhaps, with the approach of his son's wedding, he found his thoughts drifting back to his own short-lived marriage to this beautiful woman. This woman who had brought with her from her home country a bastard son, the child everyone knew but no one acknowledged.

Something in Guardin's attitude seemed . . . strange. Something in the set of his shoulders. Something Ayleth couldn't name. The hand holding the candle trembled, and at last he set the little brass candlestick down on the floor.

Then he stepped up to the painting, grabbed hold of the edge of the gilt frame, and pulled it back on its hidden hinges—hinges Ayleth now recalled noticing the first time she entered this gallery. The whole picture swung away from the wall like a door.

On the other side, Ayleth glimpsed a dark, narrow passage. Guardin picked up his candle and stepped through. The picture frame swung shut behind him, silent save for a final click.

Ayleth was left in the darkness, blinking. Wondering if

she had imagined what she just saw.

# CHAPTER 10

TERRYN WATCHED HER UNTIL SHE WAS OUT OF SIGHT. And still he stood in that shadowed doorway, his gaze following after where she had gone, half hoping, half fearing that she would reappear, that he would see her tall figure in that loose linen shift and too-large trousers hastening back toward him, the moonlight caught in her raven hair and fire sparking in her midnight eyes.

He bowed his head and forced himself to draw long, cleansing breaths. He rubbed a hand down his face, and a bitter curse burst from his lips. "Haunts damn. Haunts festering damn her!"

With a sudden growl, he turned and pounded the wall with his bare fist. When it didn't hurt enough, he pounded it again. The skin broke, and pain shot up his arm. He grimaced, closed his eyes, and let his arm go limp and fall to his side, fist clenched. He concentrated on the pain . . . but it wasn't enough.

It couldn't distract from the fire ignited within him. A fire waiting to consume him.

He knew the law. He knew these feelings were unsanctioned by the Saint. If the council of Breçar were to find out, they would bring down the gavel hard, and his career would be ruined. As yet, he'd done nothing to merit lawful execution, but . . . but . . .

He felt her in his arms. Felt the closeness of her body, the strength in her limbs, the power in her soul. A power that had seemed to lean into him. Was he . . . was he a fool for believing . . .?

Scoffing at his own idiocy, he stepped out of the alcove and strode swiftly up toward the front courtyard. It had already been a brutally long day. He was exhausted.

That was all. Just exhausted. He needed to focus his mind, focus on his work. Fendrel had given him a job, and he couldn't let himself be distracted, not by—

"We neither of us may have who we truly want."

Terryn stopped abruptly. His skin prickled at the sound of that voice, a voice he knew too well. His mouth moved, began to form a name. He whirled on his heel.

But it was Liselle who stepped out of the shadows along the castle wall and into the moonlight. "It is our sorry lot, isn't it, Venator Terryn?" she said.

His breath puffed in a long exhale at the sight of her. It was only a trick of the nerves and exhaustion that had made him think he'd heard what he could not have heard. Liselle's sweet and merry voice may be heavier than usual, weighted down with sorrow. But it was unmistakably hers.

She approached him in the moonlight, her hips swaying gently. She clutched a silk shawl tightly around her, but as she drew nearer, she let it fall back from her shoulders, revealing the wide-open neckline of a thin nightdress.

"Lady," Terryn said thickly, pulling up straight and

clasping his hands at the small of his back. "You'd best go back inside. It's bitter out tonight."

"Bitter, yes," she murmured, but continued toward him. Her hair tumbled in loose, wild curls down her back, and her eyes were hollow and dark in their sockets. He had not seen much of her in the days since the Phantom-witch's attack. He'd glimpsed her at a distance down by the lakeshore at the funeral burning of Fayline's mortal remains. Otherwise, she had been out of his sight and, truthfully, out of his thoughts as well.

But seeing her now, while the roaring fire lit in his gut still raged and his fist still smarted from pounding the wall, thoughts and sensations returned suddenly. Almost violently.

She closed the distance between them and tilted her head back to look up into his eyes. One dainty hand raised and, after a moment's hesitation, rested lightly against his cheek. "I remember," she said, "how we used to laugh about you. I remember Fayline saying that you were unbreakable, that your devotion to your saint surpassed all your natural urges. She used to dare me to see how far I could push you."

He drew a sharp breath and pulled back a step. Her lips curved, and despite the hollowness of her eyes, a remnant of her former lively smile lit up her face.

"How far, Terryn?" she said and, taking another step, slipped her arms up around his neck. Her mouth hovered just beneath his, warm and soft and willing. "How far?"

"My lady!" He pulled her hands free, but his fingers closed tight around her wrists and didn't let go, holding her arms up between their two bodies. Heat mounted inside him.

She laughed and tossed her head. "Do you think you're so subtle? I saw you with her. The venatrix, I mean. I know what you're thinking, what you're feeling. I know who it is you truly want. I don't care! Not tonight." She dropped her chin and flashed a look at him through her lashes. "Your Order forbids intimacy between members, does it not? But everyone knows you Evander-ians are more lenient when it comes to affairs of the heart outside your Order. So long as there is no . . . risk."

He let go of her wrists and took another step back, but she only drew closer to him. She caught hold of one of his hands, placed it around her waist. Her body melted against him. "Come with me," she whispered. "I'll show you what I mean. And we can forget. You can think of her, if you like. And I'll think of . . ."

Before she finished, she rose up on her toes suddenly and pressed her mouth to his. There was no softness in that kiss, no sensuality, no allure. It was a wild, angry gesture, one to which he responded in kind. He gripped her shoulders fiercely, fingers digging into her bare flesh. She caught hold of his hair, tearing and pulling. One finger trailed along the scar on his cheek, and his face jerked in response. But she held on, kissed him harder. For a few wild heartbeats, he couldn't think or feel anything but her shape, her warmth, her desire.

With a last wrench of will, he pushed her away. She staggered several paces, her silk scarf falling to the ground. Her mouth hung open, panting, and her white bosom heaved. He turned away quickly and, because he didn't trust himself, shut his eyes.

"Lady di Matin," he said, his voice ice cold and edged, "you must go back to the keep now. I have work to accomplish. We . . . nothing will happen between us. Not tonight. Not ever."

She was silent other than her heavy breathing. They stood unspeaking in the cold and the darkness, and he dared not look her way.

"So that's how it is?" she murmured at last. "You are true to your venatrix. And here I was coming to doubt that a faithful man still walked this world."

Terryn frowned. He almost shot a half glance her way, but stopped. He didn't know what she would do, and he knew he had only so much self-control remaining.

"Very well, Terryn du Balafre." He heard her footsteps coming close to him, then shivered as her hand rested on his scarred cheek. She rose on her toes again and pressed a scalding kiss to the corner of his mouth. "I honor your true-heartedness. But I'll save a dance for you tomorrow night at the very least. Don't disappoint me, your old friend."

He didn't answer. He held perfectly still, listening to the sound of her footsteps retreating. Only when he was certain she was well beyond reach did he dare turn. He glimpsed her pale form slip around a corner and out of sight.

"Haunts!" he breathed. Once more, he rubbed his face

hard with both hands. Despite the cold air, sweat beaded his brow. He'd thought he had fought all the worst battles of the flesh already! He'd thought he had learned to control and contain these desires, these urges. How could he have been so naïve? He'd thought he was made of stone.

Apparently, the chinks in that stone were deeper than he'd realized.

He shook his head and turned toward the circle drive, facing the bridge and the distant gate. He had a job to do, a spell to work. He must concentrate on his duties, his service. It was the only way. He set out with long strides, letting the wintry air cool the heat in his skin. The scar on his cheek smarted with a too-familiar pain, and he felt the place where Liselle's fingernail had traced along its puckered ridges.

Something shivered in his soul. Something he couldn't quite name.

# CHAPTER II

THE MORNING OF HALLOW'S WELL DAWNED, AND THE denizens of Wodechran Borough awoke with a sense of expectation. All eyes turned in the direction of Loch du Nóiv, and even those too far away to glimpse the towers of Dunloch Castle in the distance felt their hearts swell with hope. And trepidation.

After all, they'd celebrated this day four years ago as well . . . and it had ended in disaster.

Nevertheless, the local gentry, townsfolk, villagers,

servants, and laborers all came out to celebrate both the holy feast of Hallow's Well and, to a greater degree, their Golden Prince's upcoming nuptials. Banners flew from windows, and peasant girls tied ribbons to their hair and danced with bright-colored scarves. Bakers set to work creating golden-prince buns dripping with honey and studded with currents, which even the poorest farmhand spared a penny to buy. On this day one must indulge, one must enjoy mad moments of extravagance. On this day the prince must be toasted with wine or ale, and the new princess must be blessed with song.

One baker worked more frantically than others. He'd slept poorly the night before, and he dragged his daughter out of bed well before dawn and pushed her, still yawning, toward the donkey cart laden with many lidded baskets from which incredible aromas wafted. His daughter curled a lip, but climbed obediently into the driver's seat.

"Only a day's notice," her father muttered over and over, lifting lids and double-checking his work. "Only a day's notice . . . and for the prince's wedding feast no less! But if all goes well, it'll mean big changes for us, Meddy.

So, don't you dilly-dally along the way, d'you hear me, girl?"

"I hear'y, Pa."

"No flirting with the milk-delivery boys. No gossiping with the goose girls. You take this lot to Dunloch, then you come back straight after. I'll have the next batch ready to go then. Only a day's notice! It's madness it is. Madness. *Giyyup!*"

The baker slapped the donkey's rump, and the cart lurched into motion. His daughter settled back in her seat, guiding the donkey out of town. Her eyes lit up as she saw the banners waving, saw the signs of merrymaking already sprouting from windows and doorways. There would be a dance later in the day, and if she finished this delivery and the next one in good time, she'd get to join in. She clucked to the donkey and hurried on out of town, taking the road that led to Dunloch.

She was well on her way when a strange sound caught her ear. Frowning, she turned from her contemplation of the road between the donkey's ears and searched for the source of the noise. It sounded like a child crying and . . . sure enough, there was a grubby little girl sitting in a ditch on the side of the road, sobbing her eyes out.

"Whoa there, whoa." The baker's daughter pulled on the donkey's reins, bringing the cart to a creaking halt. Ahead of her, less than a mile off, loomed the towers of Dunloch. Her father's fine pastries cooled swiftly in their baskets, and his injunction for her not to tarry echoed in her ear. But the little girl seemed so upset.

Meddy frowned, pursing her lips. She ought to continue, she knew, but her soft-hearted nature got the better of her. She swung down from the cart and made her way to the ditch, crouching to peer down at the child. "Are'y in trouble, little'un?" she asked. "Need a hand?"

The little girl blinked huge, tear-reddened eyes up at her. "I'm sorry," she lisped, and wiped her face with the back of her hand.

Then a different voice—a strange, echoing, multitudinous voice—spoke through the child's quivering lips: "*Please forgive us, lady.*"

Meddy stood up, eyes widening. "You's . . . you's a shade-taken!" she gasped, making a sign of holy protection. "Stay away from me!"

She whirled on her heel . . . and found herself face to

face with a tall, angular woman. Her hair hung loose, her skin was scarred by hundreds of small cuts, and her nails curved long like a cat's.

"You look healthy enough," the woman said, raising her knife.

"No! No, no, please!" the baker's daughter cried. She saw the blade flash, flung up her hands . . .

But the blade never touched her. Instead, the woman plunged it into her own heart, right up under the ribs. She collapsed, convulsing with pain as blood welled up in her mouth to choke her and her shredded heart struggled to beat.

Meddy, still screaming, turned and ran down the road, leaving her cart behind. Frantic terror coursed through her limbs, blinding her to everything but the need to escape. She tripped, fell, righted herself, ran again.

Then stopped.

Her fear-twisted face relaxed, and her heart slowed its wild beating. A smile curved her lips. "Yes," she murmured. "Yes, a lovely, healthy body indeed."

"Up, up, my lady!" a sharp voice spoke directly behind Cerine's head. "It is high time we made you ready."

Startled, Cerine turned from her contemplation of the view out her bedroom window. She'd been studying the road beyond the main gate, watching how it wound away into the distance, and dreaming herself out there, running for the far horizon . . .

But she was still here. Trapped in this room, facing the coming day. And the night.

She blinked into the face of a stranger, a woman wearing an enormous pair of jeweled earrings that weighted her earlobes until they looked saggy. "Um," Cerine said, and ducked her head. "I . . . I had asked for Sister Ducette of the Siveline Sisters to come. Is she . . . is she—"

"My lady, you have no need of a *nun's* services today!" the stranger cried. "You are about to become a princess. It's high time we made you look like one." So saying, she clapped twice, and more strangers appeared as though by magic on either side of her.

Cerine responded properly and politely to the following introductions. These were all ladies of rank, chosen by the duke. Many of them Cerine had met as a girl, and some of their names she recognized. But she knew none of them. She had never been presented at court even before her retirement to Siveline . . . unlike Fayline, who'd been afforded time and opportunity to make friends among her peers.

Although her sister's name went unspoken, Cerine could almost feel the silent, negative comparisons being made as the ladies washed, polished, and perfumed her body. Aloud, they made much over her, exclaiming over her supposed points of beauty—her delicate hands and feet, her long neck, her dainty chin. They never spoke directly *to* her, merely *about* her. For this she was oddly grateful. At least no one expected her to make lively conversation.

As the afternoon dragged on, the wedding gown was brought out. Cerine, who had not seen it before, nearly choked. It was . . . enormous. She was quite certain she would smother in its multitudinous folds of silk and brocade. Every square inch of its silvery-white fabric had been embroidered with jewels and intricate patterns of gold thread, including a blazing gold sun splayed across the bodice in honor of the Golden Prince. By the time they'd stuffed her into the frilly shift, the petticoats, the panniers, the corset, and the dress itself, Cerine felt hot and exhausted. The gown was then deemed too long, so she was made to stand on a stool before a tall mirror while three ladies crawled about on the floor around her, hemming yard upon yard of silk.

Cerine stared at the reflection of herself. How odd she looked! Her hair was shaved close, a Sivelinian practice, and her eyes looked hollow in her head. In her heart she was still Sister Cerine, a novice of the temple, a scribe in training. Swathing her in silks and jewels didn't change that fact. The dress, with its wide neckline and its corsets to push her pale bosom up as high as it could go, made a valiant attempt to transform her waiflike form into something womanly and tempting.

All she could think was how much better it would have looked on Fayline.

In her mind's eye, she still saw her sister's face surrounded by lilies. Just before the flames crept up through the kindling of her pyre and consumed her, sending her ashes rising to the heavens along with the heavy scents of sacred incense.

Cerine blinked, and flames seemed to lick behind her eyelids. Only now it was a different fire blazing in her memory. The fire on a stone hearth, devouring Sister Ilda's book. Flames eating away at painstakingly written pages, curling the parchment to embers and then to ash.

She had spent all yesterday wondering if the Black Hood would come for her, if he would appear in her doorway with guards who would drag her away to the chopping block and the ax. If she would be forced to kneel, to confess her heresy to the Chosen King and his son. If she would be made to repent for daring to share it, for daring to believe it as truth.

But apparently Gerard had decided not to report her sins to his uncle. Despite everything, he still intended to go through with this farce of a wedding.

Cerine blinked at her reflection in the glass. Her insides felt hollow.

The door behind her opened, and for a moment Cerine's heart lifted as Liselle's golden head appeared in her view. Her old friend met her gaze in the glass and offered her a brilliant smile. Clad in her own finery for the ceremony and ball, Liselle was a vision of gleaming silver with amethysts ringing her throat and sparkling in her hair.

"There she is! Our blushing bride," she trilled, weaving between waiting ladies as she made her way across the room to Cerine on her stool. She held a little carved box in her hands. "A gift for you. From the prince," she said, tilting her head so that her curls fell softly across one bare shoulder.

"From . . . from the prince?" Cerine gaped. She started to reach for the box, but one of the ladies currently working on a seam tutted at her, and she froze. "Would you . . . would you mind, Liselle?"

"Of course, love." Liselle lifted the lid and held the box's contents up for Cerine's inspection. Jewels. A huge necklace of gold set with diamonds and emeralds, both a choker and a long pendant to hang down between her breasts. Earrings she could not wear, for her ears were not pierced. Two cuff bracelets that would surely break her wrists, and a headpiece to wrap across her brow.

The moment she saw them, Cerine knew Gerard had not picked this gift. This had to be her father's choice, and he'd put Gerard's name to it for appearances.

Liselle set the box aside and pulled out the choker. "Exquisite!" she said, and slipped the choker around Cerine's throat, fastening it too tight.

Cerine gasped, frowned. "Liselle, please . . ."

"I'm so sorry, dearest!" Liselle smiled and adjusted the clasp. She looped the pendant over Cerine's head next, then fastened the cuffs to her wrists like two ornate manacles. "There. Are you not magnificent?"

Cerine dared only the smallest glance in the mirror and had to look away again quickly. It was too ghastly a sight.

"Oh, come now," Liselle said with a huff and a roll of her eyes. "You look like you're on your way to your execution, not your wedding. Try to smile a little! What bridegroom wants to see his bride so sour faced?"

There was that edge to Liselle's voice again, one Cerine did not recall hearing before. But then, Liselle had been close to Fayline over the years. Cerine dropped her gaze to the floor, ashamed to meet her lady's eyes.

Liselle turned to one of the waiting ladies working furiously away at the gown's hem. Tapping her on the head, she said, "Shoo. I'll attend our princess." The lady raised an eyebrow but got up gratefully, stretching her back and flexing her fingers before she handed over both needle and thread. Liselle took her place on the low stool, selected a winking jewel from a nearby basket, and set about adding it to the hem. She worked in silence for some moments before raising a sly glance up to Cerine.

"You know, dear, as your mother is not here, I feel I must take it upon myself to offer you what advice I may. As a widow, you know, I have some experience with wedding nights."

Cerine's face went hot, then cold. She couldn't look at Liselle, and her stomach made a painful turn in her gut.

"I know you're nervous," Liselle continued. "I was myself that first night with du Matin. Though I'd had my share of little dalliances before him, a wedding night is . . . a different matter entirely. It can be rather undignified, but at least I was prepared for most of it. While you, my little duck, are as innocent as they come! So, let me tell you a few useful things."

She went on to describe in detail any number of things Cerine had never heard quite so openly discussed. Her ears burned and her pulse hammered in her throat as she tried to take in what her lady said. The more Liselle talked, the sicker she felt. She dropped her head, ashamed of what was in store for her that night, ashamed to admit the truth . . . the truth of her own desires . . .

Liselle's voice trailed off into silence at last, and she added a few more jewels to the hem without speaking. Then she reached up suddenly and squeezed Cerine's hand. "I know what you're thinking," she said.

"You do?" Cerine answered faintly.

"Of course. You're thinking about Fayline. You're thinking about how beautiful she was. You're thinking about how much Gerard loved her. He was never meant to be yours, after all." Her hand squeezed harder, almost hard enough to hurt. "But not to worry, dear girl. A man is a man. Once he's stripped you down to nothing, all he'll see is womanly flesh. He'll act on his urges then, no fear. All men are alike that way. They'll whisper of love, but once night has come, their needs are much simpler than ours and their memories much shorter."

Cerine stared at her lady, her mouth hanging open with shock. Not once in all the years she'd known her had she ever heard Liselle talk this way. Did she not realize how deeply, how excruciatingly her words cut?

"You . . . you have another you're supposed to help prepare for this evening, don't you?" Cerine asked in a small voice, hating how mousy she sounded.

Liselle's mouth curved into a too-bright smile. She tied off the last of her little jewels along the hem. "Yes," she said, snipping the thread and stowing the needle safely back in its box. "I'm to make something passably ladylike of that young venatrix. Should be an interesting challenge! But then, look what I've made of you, my dear! One looks at you and could *almost* believe one sees a princess."

Another cut. Or was it meant to be a compliment? Cerine couldn't decide. She could only feel grateful when Liselle sprang up from her stool and, wafting away in a cloud of silver silk, left the room. As soon as she was gone, Cerine realized how tight the choker necklace still was. She raised one hand to her throat, struggling to draw breath. "Please," she murmured to one of the ladies, "would you mind loosening this for me?"

The lady did as she requested and was just exclaiming that the choker was indeed much too tight and had left an indentation in Cerine's skin, when the door opened again.

Duke d'Aldreda stepped into the room.

Cerine bit back a curse.

The duke crossed the space to the mirror without a word or a look for anyone, his eyes fastened on Cerine's reflection. She watched his eyes rove up and down, his brow puckering into a critical line. He was perfectly turned out himself, in a doublet even finer than the one he had worn four years ago, his vibrant hair coiffed into a high pompadour that lent his slender figure added height.

"Where are the earrings?" he asked abruptly, turning to one of the waiting ladies.

"Her ears are not pierced, Your Grace," one of the ladies answered.

"Then pierce them."

Cerine's eyes widened in surprise. But, mercifully, one of the ladies protested for her, declaring that newly pierced ears should not carry such massive earrings, that they would bleed too much and ruin her gown.

The duke's lip curled with displeasure. "Do something about this then," he said, pointing at Cerine's shorn scalp.

Two more ladies stepped forward, carrying the elaborate headdress and veils. With no hair to pin it to, they had to strap it on under Cerine's chin. She hated it, but the duke, after scrutinizing the final result, sighed and muttered, "It'll have to do." He turned to face Cerine for the first time. Standing on her stool, she was almost tall enough to meet him eye to eye.

"You do honor to the House of Aldreda," he said. "You do honor to your sister's memory."

Cerine slowly shook her head, careful not to disturb the veils. "I don't think Fayline would see it that way."

Her father drew himself up taller. His face hardened and his jaw clenched. He took a step nearer, bringing his face close to hers.

"You will do this for *me*," he hissed. "You are the last of my house. You will be the mother of kings. *My* blood will flow in the veins of the Golden Prince's offspring. *My* blood will determine the course of history."

Cerine refused to break her father's gaze, refused to flinch, refused even to blink. She saw the desperation brimming just behind the steel of his resolve. Did he imagine this marriage of hers would somehow wash away the stains of his former enslavement? Did he believe this triumph would undo the shame he'd suffered as Inren di

Karel's plaything?

Perhaps he saw how she read his mind. Perhaps he realized how much she knew of his secret history, a history he had sought these past twenty years to obliterate. His pale face flushed with sudden rage. He left the room without another word or look her way. Cerine was left to stare at her almost unrecognizable reflection in the glass.

# CHAPTER 12

THE BAKER'S DAUGHTER PULLED THE DONKEY CART to a halt. She lifted her nose, and her eyes widened. Her head tilted slightly to one side. Inside this new host body, her unnatural senses clamored, still adjusting to the confines of these foreign limbs.

Without all the proper ceremony and procedure, body jumping was often an ugly affair. But Ylaire had done it so often by now, she'd nearly made an art form of it.

By channeling her shade's senses carefully, she

controlled this new host well enough. Ahead, her mortal eyes viewed only more of the straight paved road leading to the gates of Dunloch Castle, more of the well-tended, parklike grounds surrounding the Golden Prince's home. But her shadow perceptions detected something more.

A song spell. A barrier.

Ylaire cursed, spitting the words out into the air. Beside her in the cart, little Nilly du Bucheron shuddered and hung her head lower. The front of the child's gown was still stained with droplets of blood from the old farmwoman's host body, which now lay hidden in a ditch a quarter mile back.

The witch spared a quick glance at the girl, then focused ahead once more. She shouldn't be surprised at the presence of a barrier spell. The venators would be cautious on a day like this, even if they truly believed Inren to be dead.

Licking her host's plump, full lips, Ylaire considered. She could wait, of course. No doubt, once the wedding guests cleared out of Dunloch, once the king returned to his stronghold and the prince and his new bride had gone off on their wedding journey, the barrier would be lowered once more. She could wait until then. She'd waited all this time. What were a few more days? A few more weeks?

Too many. Even a few more hours would be far too long.

She needed to find Inren. Now.

"Stay here," Ylaire growled to the little girl, her voice sounding strange in her ears, coming through that youthful mouth. It was so good to be in a young body again! In the past she would have scorned to wear a frame so uncouth and homely, but now the strength and health of these solid limbs felt glorious.

She climbed down from the cart and led the donkey off the road, concealing beast, cart, and little girl behind a dense hedge. "I'll be a few hours," she said. "There's food in the back. Eat if you're hungry. But don't leave this cart, do you hear me?"

Nilly nodded, tears streaming down her face.

Ylaire paused briefly to consider, then dug into the pocket of her gown and withdrew the oblidite anchor. If Inren was, as Ylaire suspected, somewhere on the other side of that barrier, she'd need an anchor on this side in order to escape. Ylaire pressed the bauble into Nilly's hands. "Hold onto that," she said. "Don't let yourself or it be seen."

Nilly clutched the anchor in both small hands. Behind her tears, her eyes glimmered with shadow-light as her shade gazed out from inside her. "*I will watch over the child, Mistress,*" it said, speaking through Nilly's mouth.

"Good, Rasanala," Ylaire responded. "Don't let her run away. Unless I'm much mistaken, we're going to need this route of escape."

She left them hidden and crept on through the castle grounds, making with all stealth for that gate. She had hoped to be able to pass undetected across the bridge while wearing this new body and thereby gain access to the keep via the kitchens. Now, however, as she drew closer to the gate, that plan crumbled around her ears. The spell barrier was too strong for her to penetrate unless she attempted a very large spell involving a lot of blood, more than she could spare. And a spell that large would draw the attention of the venators on the other side of the barrier.

She peered through a curtain of willow branches

toward the gate up ahead. A venator stood guard at the entrance, inspecting every soul seeking entrance that day. Not just any venator, but a tall young man with dark skin and bright blue eyes.

A smile twisted Ylaire's lips. "The fates are with us still," she whispered through her teeth.

Then the baker's daughter stepped out from hiding and approached the gates of Dunloch on foot.

Ayleth swung the casement open, her braid falling over her shoulder as she looked down to the ground far below. Her breath caught in her throat. Had she really climbed down this way last night in the dark? And before that, days ago, while half drugged, to snatch weapons off a dead venator's body? She must be more than a little mad to have made either of those attempts. But still . . .

She lifted her gaze to the white circle drive, then beyond the bridge, across the lake waters to the far shore. There she saw curtained pavilions dotting the formal grounds of Dunloch, where those among the prince's guests not high ranking enough to merit rooms within the keep itself currently camped in semi-luxury. Anyone making a getaway from the castle would have to navigate a path through that small city of velvet curtains and fur rugs.

First, however, she'd have to find a way through the song barrier.

Ayleth strained her eyes, trying to catch a glimpse of the magic webbing with her shadow vision. But with Laranta still deeply suppressed inside her, no matter how hard she tried, Ayleth could discern not even the faintest trace of the spell she knew must even now surround Dunloch. The only possible way through was at the gate itself.

However, if she wasn't much mistaken, that was Terryn standing watch at the gate. She couldn't say for certain from this distance; his hood shielded his face. But she recognized his stance and the set of his shoulders. He seemed to be personally inspecting each and every soul that passed through those gates.

Haunts damn it all! Gnashing her teeth, she leaned a little farther out the window, considering her op—

"What do you think you are doing?"

Ayleth yelped and nearly lost her hold as Everild burst into the room. The older venatrix crossed the floor to the window in a heartbeat, catching hold of Ayleth by a handful of linen shirt and her long braid. "Get back inside, you crazed lunatic of a girl!"

"I can't go to a ball!" Ayleth wailed even as she was hauled back into the room. Laranta growled inside her, but the Suppression spells kept her down. When Everild tossed Ayleth in a heap on the floor, she hissed as stinging pain shot through the healing cuts on her torso. She scowled furiously up at the older venatrix. "There must be some mistake!"

Everild scowled right back. "No mistake. Prince's orders. Lady di Matin is due any moment to help pull you into some sort of order. Goddess knows, she's got her work cut out for her!"

While Ayleth struggled stiffly to her feet and tugged her rumpled shirt into place, Everild stomped back to the window and hauled it shut so violently, Ayleth half expected the glass to shatter. The older venatrix turned on her and pointed to the bed. "Sit. Until Lady di Matin arrives, you're not going *anywhere.*"

Everild took up a guardsman's stance between Ayleth and the door, arms folded, face closed. Slumped on the edge of the bed, Ayleth bowed her shoulders in defeat. It seemed nothing short of a miracle could save her from attending this ball. The minutes dragged past in painful silence. Several times she debated trying to draw the venatrix into conversation. Not that she particularly relished a spate of idle chatter. But she wouldn't have minded hearing voices other than those inside her head.

Her thoughts whirled like a storm, exacerbated by the closeness of the room. She kept seeing Gerard's stricken face, his smiles failing to mask his heartbreak. She kept seeing the flash of horror she'd glimpsed in King Guardin's eyes. She kept feeling Fendrel's powerful hand forcing her down onto her bed even as his shade held Laranta pinned and helpless.

She kept seeing the glint of a golden frame, candlelight flickering on its edges as it swung open on a hinge . . . and a doorway into darkness beyond . . .

She bowed her head and pressed her face into her hands, her elbows sharp on her knees. She didn't belong here. Too many mysteries surrounded her, too many bizarre and intersecting stories, none of which she understood. And her own story was the most confusing of all! She should have fled when she had the chance last night, should have knocked Terryn off his feet, dragged him into the shadows, and left him unconscious while she found a horse and fled back to the mountains and freedom—

The door opened. A bright, bell-like voice said, "I am here at last! Sorry for the delay. Lady Cerine required my assistance, but I am ready for a new challenge. Where is the venatrix?"

Ayleth looked up to see a vision of golden curls and silver silks rustle into the room, followed by five serving women, their arms mounding with frothy *things*. With ruffles.

A few paces into the room, Lady Liselle stopped short, her eyes widening as they slowly took in Ayleth, from her bedraggled braid and loose linen shirt, right down to her ill-fitting trousers and dirty bare feet. The embodiment of all things uncouth and unladylike.

Ayleth gazed sullenly back and offered no greeting.

"Behold your task, my lady," Everild said wryly. "And

may the Goddess have mercy on your soul."

"Well." The lovely woman took a few more steps, paused, and pressed a considering finger to her lips. "Hmm. I've seen worse," she decided at last.

"Worse what?" Ayleth growled. But then the foremost of the serving women spread something out on the bed, and mounds of red silk entirely captured Ayleth's attention. Bright, blood-red silk that would glow like a beacon even on the darkest of nights. Another serving woman set something that looked like a cage on the bed beside it, but by the vaguely feminine shape of the upper section, Ayleth guessed she was meant to wear it.

Her mouth dropped open. Rising to her feet, she crossed to the strange crinoline and poked at it with one finger. When the serving woman smacked at her hand, Ayleth snatched it back and clutched it to her breast. Avoiding the eyes of the beautiful golden-haired lady, she turned to stone-faced Everild. "I don't know how to . . .? Am I supposed to . . .? You can't really mean for me—"

"Don't worry." Lady Liselle stepped to Ayleth's side and took firm hold of her arm. "I'm here to help. I can get you into all of this, and if necessary I can help you back out again . . . unless you find someone more interesting to assist you, of course!" She followed this with a suggestive giggle that sent a hot flush roaring up Ayleth's neck and cheeks.

The lady then gave her a teasing pinch, dragged her to the middle of the room, and called to the serving women to help her strip Ayleth down. Ayleth cast an imploring look Everild's way, but the cold-hearted venatrix crossed her arms and assumed statue-like indifference. Only the faintest hint of a smile at the corner of her mouth betrayed her amusement.

The women hauled Ayleth's shirt over her head, and Lady Liselle squared off in front of her. As she observed Ayleth's torso, her pretty brows bunched in consternation. The shallow knife cuts had mostly healed, leaving behind ugly, puckered scars. "Oh, sweet saints above," the lady said, tapping her lips again thoughtfully. "Too bad the fashion is for such open necklines. I would almost like to add a bit of lace covering, but we can't have you looking like someone's grandmother, can we?"

"I really wouldn't mind," Ayleth said quickly, her eyes shooting again to the mounds of red silk. For the first time she took in just how open the neckline was. If "neckline" was even the word for it!

"But I *do* mind," Liselle answered. She snapped authoritative fingers, and the serving women, understanding some code Ayleth couldn't decipher, engulfed her in a flurry of activity. They pulled her hair loose from its braid and bundled her into a bath that seemed to appear by pure miracle. Ayleth couldn't remember the last time she'd bathed, not a fully submerged bath. Who had time for such luxuries when there were circuits to ride and hunts to pursue?

By the muttering of the serving women and the *tsk tsking* of Lady Liselle, it had been much too long since her last one. She was soaped, scrubbed, scraped, and scoured within an inch of her life. And these procedures were only the preliminaries. After hauling her dripping body from the bath, wrapping her wet hair, and toweling off her limbs, they proceeded to douse her in scents and salves and ointments that were so slimy on the skin, she shuddered at the touch.

"What in the Goddess's name is this made from?" she demanded as one lady aggressively rubbed something into her cheeks.

"Snail excrement," Lady Liselle answered blithely, holding up a cut-crystal bottle so that it caught the last of the fading sunlight. "I bought it from a Suurian merchant. *So* rejuvenating. They feed the snails gold leaf, and their excrement gives the skin *such* a glow! Very expensive. They say the favorite wife of the emperor of Suuria bathes in it twice daily."

"You're rubbing snail scat on my *face?*" Ayleth cast Everild another desperate look. The venatrix was definitely laughing now, hiding her mouth behind her hand.

Two women grabbed Ayleth's hands; two more claimed her feet. They picked and poked and painted even as the fifth woman attacked her hair with weapon-sharp combs and brushes. Someone heated irons on the fire, and Ayleth watched in horror as long strips of her hair were wound around these, seared into unnatural curls. She dared not pull away for fear of inadvertently branding herself.

While the women engaged in these labors, Lady Liselle set to work with pastes and creams and powders, disguising the scars across Ayleth's collarbones and even the one slicing down between her breasts. Ayleth's eyes swiveled sideways to the creation in red again. How plunging was that neckline?

Soon enough it was time to find out.

The process couldn't be a simple matter of shift, petticoat, and outer dress, of course. No, no. This was a ballgown, an invention of great complexity. The torturous garment for which Ayleth had no name was tied about her waist, suspended about her legs and posterior in a cage of bone and silk. Other items were affixed to this cage, creating even more bulk, and then something was slid around her torso and laced so tight, she had to gasp for each breath.

"You . . . *oof!* . . . can't be serious!" she protested. "How am I supposed to do *anything* if I'm slowly suffocating?"

"You're not supposed to *do* anything," Everild answered dryly. "You're supposed to stand tall and be honored. And to not embarrass anyone in front of the king."

Liselle scoffed and cast the older venatrix a disapproving glance. Then she turned a smile on Ayleth, patting her bare shoulder encouragingly. "Don't worry; the ties will loosen slightly as you dance. You'll be fine."

"I'm supposed to *dance?*"

Laranta, feeling Ayleth's distress, stirred powerfully inside her, pushing up toward the forefront of her mind. Liselle turned away, oblivious, briskly giving orders to the women to help her with the gown, but Everild took a step closer and thrust a Vocos pipe into Ayleth's hand.

"Your shade needs to be completely suppressed," she growled. "You are attending tonight as a guest, not a venatrix. If I catch even the faintest whiff of shade on you, I will personally shoot you and let you lie paralyzed in the middle of the dance floor."

Ayleth almost snapped back that she'd much prefer this to dancing, but something in the venatrix's eye made her close her mouth and accept the pipes. Everild put up a staying hand, and the waiting women stepped back while Ayleth played several variations of the Suppression Song.

*Don't send me away, mistress,* Laranta pleaded even as the spell wrapped tightly around her, dragging her down deeper than before. *Let me stay. Let me be close. I help, I help!*

*"You can't help me tonight, Laranta,"* Ayleth answered, putting a final flourish on the melody. *"No one can,"* she added dolefully.

The song spell dragged Laranta further into the pine forest of her mind, beyond Ayleth's awareness. Feeling suddenly very alone, Ayleth snapped the double-headed Vocos shut and handed it back to Everild without a word. Setting her jaw, she faced the women as they lifted the gown from the bed.

It took three of them to manipulate it over her head, and three more to arrange the layers of ruffles and pleats over the cage in which they'd trapped her. Using some sort of hook that reminded Ayleth all too much of bonehouse implements, they went about pulling laces through tiny loops and pinning things together with the most miniscule of buttons.

Ayleth shrugged uncomfortably and hauled at a sleeve, trying to pull it up into place. The women gave a collective gasp, and one of them cursed viciously. "Leave it alone!" Lady Liselle said, slapping at Ayleth's hand with real menace.

"But . . . but it's not right," Ayleth said. Then added with a sudden sinking feeling, "Is it?"

"Those sleeves are exactly where they should be, and no amount of tugging will change that. You'll only tear the dress."

Ayleth stared down, aghast. The sleeves didn't sit on her shoulders. Goddess blast it, they barely made it halfway up her upper arms! A band of red lace clung tightly across her biceps only to waft out from the elbows in a long trailing waterfall of red froth trimmed in more red lace. The bodice of the gown clung to her breasts but did little to conceal them. Ayleth suddenly hoped the women managed to get their infernal laces even tighter, because, Goddess help her, she didn't want things falling out at untoward moments!

And she was meant to appear in public like this?

"I won't be able to pass for a lady," she muttered as the serving women affixed a headpiece by driving pins into her scalp. From that circlet of red fabric, a long, gauzy veil draped down over her hair, which they'd arranged in loose curls down her back. "I won't be able to move in this thing. Much less dance or bow or—"

"Curtsy," Liselle corrected. "You curtsy in a gown like this. You certainly don't bow!" She caught Ayleth's hand and gave it a squeeze. "You'll be surprised how easily you can move. Give it a try."

One of the women coughed. When Ayleth looked her way, she saw a tall mirror that one of them had produced from some secret hiding place. Gathering up the skirts, Ayleth took a step. To her surprise, she didn't immediately fall on her face. She dared another step, and the huge contraption shifted and bounced and somehow floated across the floor.

Hesitantly she approached the mirror, not altogether certain she wanted to meet the gaze of the young woman reflected there. She fixed her eyes on her reflected feet instead. Feet clad in soft black silk slippers that just barely peeked out from under the hem. She slowly raised her gaze, noting how the understructure of the gown made her look five times as wide as she actually was.

She looked higher and winced. The copious amount of skin on display was shocking. But then again, she wasn't full-bosomed, so it wasn't as shocking as it might have been. She had to restrain herself from attempting to tug the sleeves up into what she felt should be their proper place. At a warning glance from Lady Liselle, she let them be.

Last of all she looked herself in the face. Much to her relief, it was still her own face. Somehow, she'd half wondered if these women with their strange powers would manage to change her features. But while she looked significantly cleaner, she was still basically *her*. Dark brows pinched together over equally dark eyes. Her skin gleamed with snail-gold ointment, and her cheeks had a healthy pink flush.

Ayleth scowled. "I look a sight."

Lady Liselle threw back her head and let out a peal of laughter. "My dear, you look a vision! Why, you would grace the courts of Telianor tonight. And you a heroine, at that! The young men will be flocking, positively *flocking*, I tell you."

"Goddess help me," Ayleth whispered, feeling suddenly faint.

# CHAPTER 13

"YOU'RE LATE! MY MASTER EXPECTED YOU AN HOUR ago!" the maid cried as she bolted out across the kitchen yard to greet the baker's daughter. Fists planted menacingly on her ample hips, she scowled at the young delivery girl. "This'll cost your father," she declared. "We'll not be paying full price for late pastries." Always before, the baker's daughter had driven her cart straight to the kitchen yard.

"Where are they?" The kitchen maid pressed for an

answer. "Did you lose the whole cartload?"

The feckless girl merely shrugged and pointed back toward the arched gallery passing under the west wing. A gravel track leading around the west side of the island and through the tunnel allowed deliveries straight to the kitchen door.

"Why in the Haunts-blazes did you leave it back there? Your cart lose a wheel or something?" the maid demanded.

The baker's daughter just shrugged again and turned to walk back through the tunnel, moving a little unsteadily. She'd probably been dipping into the Hallow's Well ale a bit early, the little tramp.

The kitchen maid threw up her hands and followed at a trot. "What, no excuses?" she called. "No apologies? Your father will have your hide when he finds out." The girl led her through the echoing tunnel and along the shoreline service road to a secluded stretch of the track between a stone retaining wall on one side and a drop-off down to the willow-lined lakeshore on the other. "Just how far away is your cart, you fool girl?" the maid puffed.

The baker's daughter turned to face her once more.

There was no sign of a cart or pastries anywhere. The kitchen maid stopped short, opening her mouth to curse, but the words died on her tongue when she saw what the baker's daughter held in her hand.

Blood stained the point of a long knife.

The maid's eyes widened. "What the—"

A short, sharp scream bounced from the stone wall out across the lake, swallowed up by the wind. The next instant, the maid rushed back up the track toward the castle. A spatter of blood stained her bodice, her neck, her cheek. She opened her mouth to scream again, to shout for help.

Then she stopped. Her body sagged, relaxed, drawing several deep, steadying breaths.

Minutes later, the maid entered the kitchen yard.

"Issie?" a voice called, and Gorde the footman appeared in the kitchen doorway. "Issie, is something wrong?"

The maid looked up at him and smiled, flashing all her teeth. "No, everything's fine!" she said.

"Did those missing pastries arrive yet?"

She shook her head. "No. No sign of that baker's girl

either." She took a step and staggered heavily. Gorde hurried to her side and took hold of her elbow, talking as he helped her toward the door.

No one, not even the guards on the battlements, saw the body of the baker's daughter floating face down beneath the trailing willow boughs, the gently lapping waves red with blood from a gaping wound in her throat.

Once she was certain Ayleth was presentable, Everild slipped out to finalize preparations for the evening's security. When Ayleth inquired, the venatrix answered shortly that she, Fendrel, and Terryn would all attend the festivities in uniform, mingling with the crowd, but keeping a wary eye out for any sign of shade presence. No trouble was expected; no indication had been found that the Phantomwitch was working with anyone, and no shade presence had been discovered within a twenty-mile radius of Dunloch. And, of course, the barrier spell would keep out anyone not personally verified for entrance by one of the Evanderians.

Still, it wouldn't hurt to be cautious.

Ayleth wished—so desperately wished—that she was in uniform. She remembered the conversation she'd overheard between Fendrel and Terryn the night before. Fendrel had commanded Terryn to act as her escort for the evening. Did that order still stand? Would she be forced to endure Terryn's scornful presence throughout the next few torturous hours?

How he would laugh at the sight of her! Well, not laugh, exactly. Cold-eyed Terryn probably didn't know the meaning of the word. But he would certainly be good for a dozen or more mocking comments.

Ayleth turned to the mirror, taking in the mounds of fabric, the headdress, the ridiculous, billowy sleeves. She was alone in the room with no one to stop her, so . . .

With a scowl, she took hold of first one sleeve frill, then the other. They came away at the seams around her elbows easily enough. The result was tight red sleeves down to her elbows, but without the ridiculous flapping "wings." She felt better already. But it wasn't enough.

Hiking up mounds of red silk, Ayleth managed to access the straps binding the undergarment cage around her waist. A few fumbling attempts, and the whole contraption fell to the floor. Ayleth stepped out. The layers upon layers of silk now hung from her hips to the floor like a red waterfall, rather than ballooning around her like an inflated pig's bladder. Perhaps it wasn't fashionable, but she didn't really care.

Nothing could be done about the plunging neckline or the garish color. But after she snatched the headdress from her hair and tossed it to join the cage and the sleeve frills, she felt as though she'd reclaimed some small measure of control over her life.

She waited for as long as she dared before finally opening her door, half wondering if Terryn would be waiting outside, ready to fulfill his duties as escort. No one was there, however, so she stepped out into the passage, dragging folds of red gown in her wake. Creeping along the passage, she ducked to one side and pressed against the wall whenever clusters of royal guests went by in their rich apparel. Some of these cast her curious glances in passing, but thank the Goddess, no one tried to speak to her.

She progressed in this halting, hesitant fashion until she finally made it to the open rail overlooking the entrance hall. Down below, all was lit to brilliant gold by a thousand candles reflecting off ladies' jewels and gentlemen's bright buckles. The beautiful wedding guests milled about in a dense rustle of skirts, murmuring polite conversation as they waited for the evening's ceremony to officially begin.

Ayleth blinked several times. Somehow, she couldn't quite shake from her memory the vision of six days ago, when she had gazed out from this same hiding place into this same vast space. Then, instead of smiling guests in wealthy finery, the floor had been crowded with cowering hostages. And the Phantomwitch had paced up and down between them, ready to kill anyone who looked at her the wrong way.

But the witch was dead. Ayleth squeezed her eyes shut, turning her head away. When she looked again, she forced those visions down inside her. The witch was dead. The prince was safe. And she was here as a guest, not a venatrix.

At a sudden fanfare of trumpets, Ayleth ducked further behind her pillar, heart thudding, and peered around the marble only just in time to see a procession making its way toward the staircase from the west wing, opposite her hiding place. Beautiful ladies clad in gold led the way, followed by a cluster of Siveline nuns in blue hoods. Last of all came the tall figure of Duke d'Aldreda, unmistakable with his elegantly coiffed red hair. And on his arm could be none other than the prince's bride, Lady Cerine herself.

Ayleth narrowed her eyes. Then she nearly choked on a gasp. "The novice!" she whispered. Of all people, it was the same pale-faced girl she had rescued in the ruins of Cró Ular. The one who had assisted in her battle against the Phantomwitch. She had been Gerard's intended bride all along? Well, that explained a few things.

But . . . O Goddess above! How many times and in how many ways had she managed to make a fool of herself in front of this lady? Embarrassment burned Ayleth's cheeks, and she was grateful for the pillar to hide behind.

Gerard waited at the foot of the staircase, clad in a gold-trimmed white suit of some kind, his garments a perfect match for Lady Cerine's. An elegant, diamond-studded headdress and veil covered the bride's head, and she certainly didn't look like a temple scribe anymore. She looked like a true princess, royal and regal in bearing.

Ayleth watched as the duke led his daughter down the stairs and handed her over to the handsome prince. She continued to watch as the prince led his bride through the parted crowd and the procession made its way to the front doors, led by priestesses and incense bearers. The king himself walked at his son's right hand, and the Black Hood kept pace just behind. They passed through the doors and continued out into the torchlit evening, heading down to the shores of Loch du Nóiv, where the Rite of the Holy Well would take place.

If Ayleth was to bear witness, she needed to hurry. But the temptation was strong to stay right where she was. Surely Gerard wouldn't notice her absence amid all that mighty company? But while Gerard would not, Everild certainly would. And she would come hunting.

With a sigh, Ayleth drew herself together. Like it or not, it was time to be *honored*.

The entrance hall was empty by the time she made her tentative way along the railing toward the head of the stairs. All the guests had filed out behind the wedding procession. Perhaps she could creep down and keep to the back of the crowds all night. Perhaps once she'd watched a dance or two, she could even sneak away. With these thoughts bolstering her courage, Ayleth gathered the front of her skirts and took the first step down. The stairs seemed to loom large and dangerous, and she had an altogether too vivid image of tripping and tumbling all the way to the bottom.

Laranta, bound deep though she was, seemed to sense the image and uttered a low, chuckling growl. *"Hush, you,"* Ayleth growled back. Putting out one hand, she clutched the polished stair rail. One step, two.

Someone moved down below. Though she should have kept her focus fixed on the next step down, Ayleth shifted her gaze almost against her will. Terryn stood at the base of the stairs, looking up at her. His eyes were so cold, she felt his gaze freeze her skin. All of her skin. All of her terribly exposed skin . . .

"Haunts damn!" she yelped as her foot caught against the hem of her skirt and she staggered the next two steps. Clutching the rail, she felt the laces and boning of her corset strain, and listened for some telltale rip. Thank heaven, she'd removed the massive undercarriage! It certainly would have ruined her balance and sent her crashing all the way to the floor below. She pushed herself upright again, adjusted the fall of her long skirts, then trained a ferocious scowl Terryn's direction.

He didn't speak. He didn't move.

*"You'd look ridiculous in a ballgown."*

The memory of his words the night before rang in her ear. She felt her skin burning and could only hope he would mistake it for the rosy glow cast by candlelight. Recovering her dignity as best she could, she continued down the staircase. Her confidence rose with each step.

When she arrived at the last three steps, Terryn bowed with solemn dignity. The elegant bow of a courtier, not the crisp, neat bow of a venator. "Venatrix di Ferosa?" he said and offered a gloved hand.

Ayleth gave the hand a look, making no move to take it. "What?" she demanded. Her traitorous mind flashed a memory of that same hand pressed against the small of her back, holding her close, so close she could feel the beat of his heart. But she made absolutely certain no trace of those thoughts showed in her face as she lifted her gaze to his.

One dark eyebrow crooked. "It is customary for a lady such as yourself to be escorted at formal occasions." His eyes focused hard upon her face. Too hard. Something about the intensity of his stare made her much more aware of all the exposed skin at which he refused to glance. "You look as though you might not make it without help," he added.

She took the last three steps unaided, gazing pointedly ahead. Out of the tail of her eye, she thought she saw his eyes flick down and up again, but she wouldn't give him the satisfaction of noticing. "Don't you have a job to do tonight?" she asked in a voice as icy as his.

Terryn drew a breath through his nostrils. Then, before she could duck out of his reach, his hand darted out, caught hold of hers, and tucked it under his elbow. "I do," he said. "My job is to keep an eye on you. And I intend to fulfill my duty to the utmost of my abilities."

She yanked, but he held on tight. She could have broken free easily enough. Even without Laranta's strength, she knew a few quick turns that would leave him arm-twisted and gasping for mercy on the floor. But

Terryn bent his head and hissed in her ear, "At least *try* to play the part of a lady. For Gerard's sake."

His breath tickled her skin. The nearness of his lips to her ear sent a jolt straight to her gut. For a few breaths she couldn't think of anything. Her mind scrambled with sudden and unexpected sensations, sensations for which she had no name.

She shivered and pulled back a step, letting a lock of her loose hair fall over her shoulder as a flimsy protection. He was right, of course. She didn't know the protocols and expectations of a night like this. Terryn did. It would behoove her to follow his lead. But she needed to keep her head on straight, needed to maintain a certain distance between them.

"All right, du Balafre," she said, her voice a little higher and tighter than usual. "Lead on."

# CHAPTER 14

CERINE WAS GRATEFUL FOR THE VEIL SHE WORE OVER her face, thin though it was. It felt like some protection from all those watchful eyes as she moved at the front of the procession down to the shores of the lake. The sun had already mostly set, leaving only a stain of russet light along the western horizon at their backs. The wedding company faced east toward the moon rising large and red over the trees. It cast a shimmering glow across the water, like a path to heaven itself.

She felt Gerard's gaze dart to the side of her face. Her hand trembled in his grasp, and though she wanted to pull away, to separate herself from him, she depended on his support. Without him, her knees would buckle, and she'd fall in a disgraceful heap.

Grand Mother Didienne, as high priestess of Siveline Temple, conducted the Rites of the Holy Well. Though the night was cold, and she required the assistance of two priestesses to assist her, she stepped right down into the lake water. Her elegant robes wrapped about her fat, shivering knees, and her elaborate headdress swayed heavily with every move she made. But the old woman had experience with this sort of discomfort. Four years ago, she had stepped into these same moonlit waters on a similarly cold night. And she had beckoned Fayline to her even as she beckoned Cerine now.

Cerine let go of Gerard's hand as the two of them approached the edge of the lake and stood with the water just lapping at their feet. The edge of her white wedding gown was dampened, but she didn't care. Neither did she feel the cold wind blowing in her face. She scarcely heard the prayers Mother Didienne sang over her and the prince.

Instead, Cerine's attention focused on that faintly wavering reflection of the moon.

On this night, once every year, the waters of Loch du Nóiv became the sacred Holy Well. It was here that the Goddess was said to have stepped down from heaven itself to speak to her first Priestess Queen. And she had taken that young woman's hand and placed it in the hand of her greatest enemy, the prince of the neighboring kingdom, who had vowed to kill her and her people. The Goddess bade them be united in love, joining their nations. The prince, struck by the glory of the Goddess, knelt in those waters and vowed his loyalty to her and to her priestess. Thus, the two warring kingdoms became one, and Gaulia was formed. For centuries after, tradition saw the Priestess Queens of Gaulia come to Loch du Nóiv to be anointed on the night of the Holy Well along with those consorts they had chosen for themselves.

The Priestess Queens were no more. The time of kings was now at a hand, a new order under the will of the Mother Deity. But when the High Priestess of Liane had declared that Guardin du Glaive's son would be wed on Hallow's Night on the shore of Loch du Nóiv, all were pleased by this mirroring of ancient traditions.

So Cerine stood in Fayline's place, here on the bank of the sacred lake, where four years before she'd stood as part of the crowd, murmuring responsive prayers in unison with the rest of the gathering. Now, she listened to those responses behind her and shivered as though hearing the echoing whispers of ghosts reaching out from the past.

The ceremony drew to its close. "Face one another, my children," Grand Mother Didienne said, motioning sharply with quavering hands.

Cerine turned to the prince. He wore white, even as she did—the traditional color of a Holy Well wedding. White trimmed in gold, as befit the Golden Prince. The cut of his jerkin and the sweep of his elegant half cape made his shoulders look even broader than they were, and the wide belt only emphasized the trimness of his narrow waist. His hair, usually tossed about his face in boyish golden curls, was slicked back, exposing his broad, pale forehead and the fine, clear-cut bones of his cheeks and jaw. He looked older than his twenty-two years.

And behind his smile she could see the never-distant sadness.

Cerine quickly dropped her gaze and focused on his chin. But she felt the intensity of his eyes fixed on her.

At last Mother Didienne clapped her old hands together and intoned, "What the Goddess sees fit to join, let neither soul nor shade tear asunder!"

Cerine saw Gerard's jaw clench. Those same words had been spoken over him and Fayline . . . and hours later, as they danced in celebration of their union, she was torn from his arms, never to be reclaimed.

But the assembly on the lawn chorused the "Amen," nearly drowning out Didienne's muttered, "Now someone get me out of this pond. Where is my robe?" The sacred instruments began to play the solemn hymn to which Gerard would lead his bride back inside for the commencement of the festivities. Gerard reached for her hand, but she only let him touch the barest tips of her fingers as she turned to face the gathering.

She caught her father's eye. Duke d'Aldreda, his mouth smiling, his one good eye hard as flint, speaking silent injunctions with every breath he took.

*You have a duty to your family.*

*You must honor your sister's vow.*

*You have one purpose in this life.*

*Legacy of kings . . . promise of the Goddess . . .*

Cerine set her chin and moved beside Gerard through the throng. They passed back into a castle alight with hundreds of candles casting the moldings and window treatments into a golden haze. Garlands of paper flowers guided them through the passages to the ballroom itself. The doors stood wide open to receive them, and Cerine heard the strains of musicians warming their instruments.

They stepped into the room beneath the glittering gold-wrought chandeliers, their images reflected on the high polish of the inlaid floor. Cerine paused just inside the doorway. Through her mind flashed a too recent memory: the memory of her sister dancing in the middle of that floor, her head thrown back in laughter.

Then blood.

Then screams.

And a bolt of pure, poisonous darkness.

"Cerine?" A gentle voice called her back to the present.

Startled, Cerine blinked and forced herself to meet Gerard's gaze.

"Will you do me the honor of a dance?" he asked. His smile was as sweet as a spring dawn.

Cerine nodded wordlessly but could not find the will to answer his smile with a smile. Sensing her discomfort, Gerard took both her hands in his, squeezing gently as he led her to the middle of the floor.

"It's all right," he whispered. "We've just got to get through the first dance. That's all."

The guests poured into the room, lining the walls, filling in spaces between the tall candle stands and the tables of refreshment. Cerine felt the weight of their eyes on her. How she longed for the musty quiet of the temple scriptorium! How she longed for the shielding comfort of her novice's hood. The thin veil she wore over her face offered no real protection from all those eyes.

A song began to play, lilting and sweet. Gerard put his hand about her waist, leading her in the first pattern across the floor. Her skirts whispered softly about her feet, disguising how many steps she missed as she followed her prince's lead. It had been so long since she'd danced! But Gerard, graceful as a swallow in air, led her nimbly, making up for her deficiencies with his experience.

The first pattern complete, Gerard moved Cerine into the second, which drew them closer together, facing one another. She met his gaze for an instant before lowering her eyes to study the pattern of embroidery across his chest. Her foot missed a step, and she stumbled, but he caught her, steadied her . . . and pulled her closer.

Hastily Cerine pushed back, putting distance between them. Her heart hammered in her throat, and she tucked both lips between her teeth, biting down hard.

Liselle's voice floated in the back of her head: "*Not to worry, dear girl . . . once he's stripped you down to nothing, all he'll see is womanly flesh. He'll act on his urges then, no fear.*"

"Cerine." Gerard's voice was a low undertone beneath the light, soaring music. "Cerine, I want you to know . . . I need you to know . . ."

She shook her head, her brow knotting. Why could she not stop the frantic beating of her heart? The prince's hand pressed against the small of her back, pulling her near enough that she almost believed she could feel his heartbeat as well. She knew she should resist, and yet she couldn't bear to. She let him draw her in, let him put his head close to hers.

"Whatever else you think of me," he whispered, "whether you believe me to be a fraud or a fake . . . I want you to know that I am no liar. I meant every word of that letter I wrote."

The pattern of the dance required him to spin her. Cerine gasped for breath as she whirled out in a flurry of skirts. But then she was pulled close once more, the reprieve all too short.

"Please, Cerine," he said, trying to catch her eye. "I understand if you don't feel the same way after . . . after everything. But I want you to believe—"

"No." Cerine forced herself to look at him, to meet his gaze steadily. "Don't say anything more. Not now."

Hurt flashed through his eyes. But he spun her again, and when he drew her gently back, his face was a perfect, pleasant mask.

The song ended. The guests applauded. And the prince bowed while his bride sank into a deep curtsy. Then, thank the Goddess above, he led her to a chair and let her sit. He moved away into the crowd, out of her sight, and Cerine folded her hands, bowed her head, closed her eyes . . . and prayed to the Goddess that she would have the strength to resist.

She dared not believe Gerard's declarations. They could not be true. No matter how she might wish it, they *could not be true.* Cerine was now his wife, and she would be a good wife. She would be loyal, faithful, and loving insofar as she dared. In a few short hours, she would let herself be led to his room, led to his bed, and she would fulfill all that was required of her.

But she must never let herself believe that Gerard would love anyone but Fayline. Or her heart would surely break in two.

# CHAPTER 15

MOTHER DIDIENNE EASED DOWN INTO THE CHAIR provided, panting and groaning as her fragile limbs cracked in protest. "Where is Sister Julene?" she snapped when a young sister whose name she did not recall entered the room, carrying a beautiful—and, more to the point, *dry*—robe over one arm.

The young sister nodded respectfully and set the robe aside across the back of a nearby chair. "Sister Julene is indisposed tonight," she said. "I will attend you in her stead. Would you like to be made ready for the ball, Grand Mother?"

"I would *like* to be made ready for bed," Didienne answered with a growl. She held up a scrawny, flabby arm for the young priestess to help her out of her soaking ceremonial garments. She was getting too old for this sort of thing. The prince had better stay married this time, because if she had to come back and perform one more Hallow's Night ceremony, it would surely be the death of her. "But I will honor the Chosen King and make an appearance, I suppose," she muttered.

The young sister knelt at her feet with a towel to dry off any residual dampness. Didienne peered down at her with bleary eyes. The wrinkles on her brow pulled together in a frown.

"Is that . . . young woman, is that *blood* I see on your hand?"

The sister held up her hand, her expression surprised. Then she blinked up at the older woman and smiled wanly. "Why, yes. Yes, it is, Grand Mother. Would you look at that?"

A flash of steel, and a knife slipped from the depths of

her sleeve.

"Goddess save us!" Didienne cried, springing to her feet.

She was going to die. Slowly. Painfully. And imminently.

The music, the glitter, the press of people, the mingling of a thousand perfumes. It was too much! Ayleth's senses revolted, and she stopped as though frozen in the doorway of the ballroom, her heart beating so furiously, she couldn't find the will to move.

Overhead, golden chandeliers dripped with light and beads of white wax. The marble floor was polished to such a sheen, it reflected the movement of the dancers like a mirror. The tall windows along one wall were open to let in a breeze, otherwise the heat of so many bodies pressed together would have been too much, particularly for the ladies who, like Ayleth, strained against the laces beneath their gorgeous gowns.

"Don't stand gawking," Terryn whispered, his mouth once more too near her ear for comfort. She shivered but forced herself not to flinch. "Smile and follow my lead."

Much to her surprise, he added, "You'll be all right."

Was that actual encouragement? From Terryn du Balafre? This was a night of miracles!

He moved her into the ballroom, passing various knots of lords and ladies, who eyed her with mild curiosity. Despite the extreme redness of her gown and the overabundance of skin she had on display, Ayleth realized that she did blend into the company rather well. Many of the women wore gowns far more revealing than hers, and they laughed and flirted and danced without a thought, calling attention to themselves with batted eyes and daintily shrugged shoulders. If she kept her mouth shut and clung to the shadows, she might be able to disappear.

Now, if only she could separate herself from Terryn. Because while she might manage to slip into the shadows and disappear, Terryn stood out like a sunflower among daisies in his venator uniform. He was already much taller than most of the men in the room, and his uniform included a dramatic red sash across his chest, which attracted every female eye as they passed. Several of those female gazes fixed on Ayleth as well, taking the measure of the girl who clung to the arm of the handsome venator.

An uncomfortable irritation knotted in Ayleth's gut. Every one of those women assumed she was just another frill-clad miss vying for Terryn's attention. Not one of them saw her for what she really was: Terryn's competition and a viable threat to his future.

Ayleth dropped Terryn's arm and pried her hand out of his grasp, using a little more force than she wished to free herself. He looked at her sharply, opening his mouth to protest. Before he could say a word, a hand glittering with rings landed on his arm.

"Venator Terryn! We meet again." Lady Liselle tossed golden curls back from her pristine white shoulders as she glided close to Terryn's side. She cast Ayleth a smile, looking her up and down. "And the venatrix, of course. Looking . . . not quite how I left you." A faint frown puckered her brow as she took in the fall of Ayleth's skirts, noting the lack of cage-like undergarments. But she disguised the frown quickly, flashing another smile. "Are you finding those slippers comfortable? You'll be light as a feather for dancing."

"Oh, I won't dance," Ayleth answered quickly, shaking her head.

Liselle shook her head and laughed, her eyes sparkling, though for the life of her, Ayleth couldn't figure out what she had said that would inspire such mirth. "But what of you, Venator Terryn?" the lady said, turning to Ayleth's escort. "Are you equally determined to stand by the wall tonight? Or will you show all these pretty palace boys what a real man can do when the right tune is playing?"

Terryn glanced sideways at Ayleth. She looked back, raising her eyebrows, and noted how his dark skin flushed. So. This Lady Liselle and he . . . knew each other. Ayleth tilted her head slightly, her mouth quirked in a smile. Interesting.

"Come, Terryn," Liselle persisted as the musicians struck up another tune. "This is one of your favorites, if I remember correctly. Come, dance with me."

"I, uh . . ." Terryn looked at Ayleth again. But Lady Liselle applied a little force to her grip, and Terryn caved, allowing himself to be led to the dance floor. Ayleth watched him go, her mouth still smiling. She felt as though she'd just had a glimpse into the private life of her competitor, a complex life that involved people and places she knew nothing about. It was interesting. It was . . . Her smile slipped into a frown. It was odd. Odd to discover how little she really knew this man with whom she had fought and hunted and served and bickered these last several weeks.

Odd to realize that there were other women in this world with whom he shared history. More history than existed between the two of them, that was for sure.

Realizing she should take advantage of her current freedom, Ayleth slipped through the crowds, seeking shelter across the room behind a potted tree. Once safely ensconced behind its garlanded boughs, she peered back out at her nemesis on the dance floor, whirling in a complex pattern with his lovely dance partner.

If Ayleth had considered her own dress revealing, Liselle's was practically falling off. Ayleth couldn't imagine being comfortable out in public wearing such an ensemble of froth and nothing, but somehow Liselle made it look easy. She moved with utmost grace and confidence, fully aware of her attributes, fully aware of how every man in the room struggled not to look where he shouldn't, and using this to her advantage.

Terryn's gaze fixed hard on his partner's face—on her forehead, if Ayleth judged correctly. Liselle talked animatedly, and Ayleth saw him nod and offer responses. He spun her out from him in a flurry of silver skirts, then pulled her back close.

Ayleth's stomach twisted.

She frowned and looked away quickly. Nerves, she told herself. She was just a bundle of nerves tonight. She needed something steadying. A refreshment table beckoned, and she decided to risk leaving the shelter of her potted tree to move around the periphery of the room. Soldiers lined the walls at intervals, solemn men in uniform with their sharp lances prominently displayed. The king's personal guard, un-taken men who couldn't hope to stand up against a shade-taken, but fierce-looking fellows, nonetheless. They lent the room a sudden air of solemnity, despite the music and the laughter and the fine food and wine. Ayleth slid past one of the guards and, to her surprise, found herself quite close to Lady Cerine.

The young woman sat quietly in a chair a little apart from the crowd, her hands folded in her lap. She certainly did not look like the bride she was, newly joined in marriage to the Golden Prince, destined to be the nation's queen. Her expression was closed off behind her veils, and her gaze fixed upon her folded hands. Diamonds and gold flashed around her throat but somehow contrived to look more like shackles than jewelry.

Ayleth stopped. Should she speak to the lady? They had met several times, though never officially. A vague memory of clutching at a woman's skirts and slurring threats plucked at the back of Ayleth's mind. She hastily shook that away, but she couldn't quite summon the courage to approach. Instead, she withdrew to her tree and looked around for another angle she might take to reach the refreshments.

The king was watching her.

Ayleth met his gaze all the way across the room, through the whirling pattern of dancers. Guardin sat above the gathering on an upraised dais at the far end of the room. Dominus Fendrel stood at his elbow, square and stern, studying the dancers as though any one of them might transform into an enemy in the blink of an eye. But the king watched Ayleth.

Her blood turned to ice. She shouldn't be here. She shouldn't be in the same room as this man. Whatever he had against her, whatever he saw when he looked at her . . . she didn't want to know.

"I think that's enough *honoring* for one night," she muttered, and turned toward the door with half a mind to leave the ball entirely, to cut herself free of this Haunts-damned dress, to flee to the stables and make her escape once and for all. She needed to—

"You look like a lady in great need of a dance."

Startled, Ayleth turned and found herself face to face with a young man, his features framed by curls tousled rather too perfectly. He grinned at her, his smile wide enough to fill the whole room, and his eyes glittered as they moved obviously and admiringly across her figure. Ayleth barely stopped herself from folding her arms over her breast.

"I don't believe we've met yet," the young man said with a courtly bow, flourishing one hand. "I am Srian, Comte du Landriard. And whom do I have the pleasure of addressing?" He caught her hand in his as he spoke, drawing her fingers to his lips. She wanted to pull away.

But she was a guest of the prince. She should at least try to act like a lady.

"Ayleth," she answered, and on impulse added, "Venatrix di Ferosa."

"Venatrix?" The young man didn't relinquish her hand, though his voice caught with surprise. Then he smiled again, and his thumb moved up and down across her knuckles. With practiced ease that spoke of many years' experience in courtly intrigues, he drew her gently toward him. "I've never danced with a venatrix before. Tell me, are you armed with a dozen lethal poisons even as we speak?"

Ayleth's mouth dropped open. "Where would I fit poisons in a rig like this?" she blurted. And then blushed. How was she supposed to navigate such an encounter? She didn't know any of the rules. Was she supposed to flirt? How did one flirt, exactly? Un-taken folk usually looked on her with terror the moment they learned what she was.

Sensing that conversation wasn't her strong suit, the young man took a different tack. He placed a familiar hand around her waist and guided her toward the dance floor, still smiling, still talking with ease. "I've heard many an interesting tale of Evander's loyal female followers over the years," he said. "But I've never heard of any venatrix being quite so bewitching. Had I known the possibilities, I should have enlisted in the Order myself!"

Ayleth flushed again. It was an appalling line, but she couldn't help herself. Heat rushed up her neck. "That's not how it works," she muttered. But this didn't seem to matter to the young man. In something of a daze, Ayleth found herself led right to the edge of the dance floor, and in another few paces, she'd be drawn into the dance.

Fear of an entirely new variety bloomed in her heart. She stopped as though her companion were trying to drag her to the brink of a chasm. She tried to pull away, but his grasp was persistent. Five different ways she could apply pressure to his joints and bring him crumpling to his knees played across her mind in quick succession. But she couldn't do that . . . could she? No, no, this man was the prince's guest!

"What's wrong, gentle venatrix?" the young comte asked with another smile that threatened to blind her with its brilliance. "Does this song not please you?"

Nothing pleased her, nothing at all. But though she opened her mouth, she couldn't find an excuse. What could she say? How could she admit that she had no idea how to dance this or any of the dances she saw being performed? All those intricate steps and turns and weavings in and out . . .

"I feel a little faint," she said. It wasn't entirely a lie. Dread of that dance floor gripped her harder even than the incorrigible comte, and the laces of her gown seemed suddenly much too tight.

Her companion wasn't so easily convinced. "Don't be shy," he said with another forceful tug. "I'll guide you through the steps, and soon you'll see—"

"I believe the lady said she was faint."

The icy voice shot over Ayleth's head to pierce the Comte du Landriard between the eyes. The young man blenched and dropped his hold on her, looking up and over her shoulder.

Ayleth wanted to curse. She knew that voice. It was the last voice she wanted to hear coming to her rescue.

"Your pardon, Venator du Balafre," the young comte said, bowing, this time without any flourishes. "The lady and I were—"

"Enough." Terryn took a step closer. She could feel his looming presence behind her, the warmth of his body contrasting with the coldness of his voice. "Go find someone else to bother."

The comte cast Ayleth one last look, but it was brief. The next instant, he was lightly making his way across the dance floor as the most direct route of escape, dodging between couples and headed for the other side like a knight on horseback forging a raging river.

"I didn't need your help," Ayleth muttered without turning. If she had any luck left to her, Terryn would sidle away as silently as he'd sidled up behind her. "I had the situation under control."

Rather than removing his offensive presence, Terryn stepped to her side. He stood easily in his dress uniform, his right hand gripping his left wrist at the small of his back. If only a lady might assume that stance! Ayleth couldn't figure out what she was meant to do with her elbows.

"You must dance tonight," he said. "It will be much too conspicuous if you don't."

"I don't see why everyone is so concerned about whether I dance or not," Ayleth answered curtly. "No one will notice one way or another."

The musicians in the gallery overhead ended their melody. Ayleth watched the couples on the floor whirl in a last complex configuration, arms upraised and crossed in a pattern she would have to watch from above to understand. She wondered if she could slip up to the gallery for a better view.

"There you are mistaken," Terryn said.

"What?" Ayleth looked up at him. As the dancers made their way off the floor, flowing past the two of them, he took a step closer to keep from being separated from her in the sudden press of people. He stood so close their arms brushed, and when he looked straight down at her, she could see the gleam of fire deep in the center of his black pupils.

"I said you are mistaken," he repeated. In the sudden influx of conversation from the dancers, Ayleth had to study his lips, reading the words he spoke rather than hearing them. "You're mistaken if you think you'll escape notice. You can't help but draw every eye in this room."

Ayleth could think of no answer. And her eyes were still fixed on his mouth.

A new song floated down from overhead. It began in a low, creeping cadence, like evening shadows drawn along by beckoning woodwinds. A melody that called to the deep places inside the soul, like a spell song. Only this song was of mortal making, intended for mortal ears, mortal souls. And mortal enchantments.

Terryn took her hand. Somewhat to her own surprise, Ayleth didn't resist as he led her in among the other couples lining up on the dance floor. His eyes never left hers, and when she gave a sudden gasp, realizing where she stood, he said, "Don't worry. This one is simple enough. I will guide you."

The drums began a rhythmic beat, gentle but profound, in time with the woodwinds. Then the single, plucking, low-note string of a lute sang out the paces of the dance. Terryn held both Ayleth's hands in his, lifting them up as he led her in the first turn. Her full skirts flared like wings or flames without the caging undergarments to hold them demurely in place, and Ayleth felt suddenly transformed into something wild and dangerous. A bird of fire.

And did that make Terryn the hunter trying to catch her in his snare?

Ayleth smiled suddenly, fiercely. The dance music flowed into her soul like a Vocos song, and she understood its call. It was not a summoning of control, but a call to battle. And she never backed down from a fight.

Her feet found the paces, guided by Terryn, but only for the first turn. Then she started to improvise, pulling away from him. She broke the pattern followed by the other dancers, but it didn't matter. They continued without her, and she created her own new design, weaving in and out among them, red wings flying. She darted, floated, and came back to Terryn, this time without touching his hand, breast to breast, face to face, a mere inch of air between them.

The music called. She turned to answer, but he caught her around the waist, pulling her back to him before she broke the pattern again. And they were suddenly alone in the center of the dance, turning in time to the drumbeat, his one hand holding her at the small of her back, the other upraised.

A victory for him. But not for long.

Ayleth's smile grew. She watched his expression falter at the sight. He knew he had met a worthy combatant. The other ladies, they didn't understand this dance. Not another soul understood it. They gave themselves willingly to their partners' leads, floating gracefully like so many kites on their tethers. But Ayleth was no kite. She was a firebird, and she would fly free.

The song rushed suddenly in a burst of darkness, punctuated by pinpricks of starlight strings. Ayleth raised her arms over her head and, with a single twirl, broke Terryn's hold. He didn't quite release her from his orbit, however, moving first opposite to her and then back into the pattern. The other dancers formed circles, and Ayleth joined one of these, letting the flowing rhythm carry her away from Terryn. But the circle must round back eventually.

And there they were again, face to face just as the final notes of the song broke like a sunburst through the dark melody and ended in a glorious clap of brilliance.

Ayleth's chest heaved with exertion as her lungs struggled against the tight laces. To her surprise, Terryn looked winded as well, breathing hard through flaring nostrils. A quick glance from side to side told her that the other dancers had not found the dance quite so strenuous. They clapped politely, smiling at their partners, the men offering the ladies their arms as they led them from the floor.

Terryn did not offer his arm. He spoke in a voice that rumbled deeper than the drums, "That is not how that song is meant to be danced."

"Maybe not," Ayleth answered, grinning wickedly up at him through her labored breathing. "But that's how I dance it."

Her battle won, she pivoted on her heel and left him where he stood.

# CHAPTER 16

FLANKED BY TWO PRIESTESSES CLAD IN GORGEOUS, holy raiment, Grand Mother Didienne entered the ballroom. The royal guests parted before her, bowing as though to a queen, and she moved with great dignity through them, nodding here, making a sign of blessing there. Having left her rowan-wood cane behind in her dressing room, she leaned for support on the arm of a sister instead, silently cursing the frailty of her body with every step she took.

She should have found a younger, stronger host. But no host in all of Dunloch was less likely to draw the suspicion of those Haunts-damned venators.

Her small procession made its way to the dais where King Guardin sat in glory above the merrymakers. At his side stood his brother, Fendrel du Glaive. The shriveled old heart hidden inside Mother Didienne's breast throbbed with hatred at the sight of them.

*Hush,* she whispered to that secret power she held suppressed deep at the core of her spirit. *Don't attract our enemy's attention. We're not here for vengeance. Not tonight.*

The spirit inside her obeyed, bowing its head and curling into a silent coil of nothing, too small to attract the attention of even the most sharp-eyed venator.

"Grand Mother," King Guardin said, extending a gracious hand to the old priestess as she presented herself before his throne. "You and the Sisters of Siveline honor us tonight with your presence. I am personally grateful that you should travel all this way to officiate the wedding of my son."

"All to the glory of the Chosen King and his house," Mother Didienne answered, though the words were poison on her tongue. She bowed her head deeply then squeezed the arm of the priestess she held, urging her to back them away from the dais once more.

A seat had been prepared for the high priestess off to the left of the king's dais, and she gratefully sank into this, resting her weary body. Cursing silently in the privacy of her head, she vowed to rid herself of this aged husk at the first opportunity. But for now . . . for now, the disguise was too good to pass over.

Leaning back in the chair, she looked out through bleary eyes, studying the merrymakers in the room. Her eye was drawn particularly to a tall figure on the dance floor, handsome in a red sash and uniform. Her lips curled in a bitter smile.

"My pretty little slave," she murmured.

"What was that, Grand Mother?" One of the priestesses standing at attendance beside her bowed, her face mildly concerned. "Do you need something?"

"No, no." Didienne waved the woman away and settled more comfortably in her chair. Though her gaze kept drifting back to the young man, she forced herself to study every other face in that room.

*Where are you, Inren?*

That which lurked inside Didienne's mortal body had thought long and hard over the words pried from Terryn's unwilling mouth. She refused to believe it. Inren, overpowered by Duke d'Aldreda's daughter, recklessly attacking castle guests and then getting herself killed by some green young venatrix? No. Inren was too smart, too sly. Yes, she might temporarily be saddled with the soul of the duke's idiot daughter. But Inren herself wouldn't go into a fight without proper precautions.

*You're here somewhere,* the Warpwitch whispered deep inside her withered host body. *I know you're here. Come out of hiding and reveal yourself to me . . .*

"Your friend is full of surprises tonight, is he not, good prince?"

Gerard started a little at the voice speaking suddenly at his side, diverting his attention from the dance floor. He looked down at Lady Liselle, who offered him a smile. He nodded in return, then turned his gaze back to the dance, watching Ayleth whirl in a storm of red fabric while

Terryn stood his ground, pulling her back every time she seemed ready to fly free. There was a look in the venator's eye that Gerard could not remember seeing there before. And Ayleth's face . . . now, that was a sight, indeed!

"It takes a brave man to dance with a venatrix," Gerard said with a wry grin, leaning his shoulder against a garland-wrapped pillar. "A braver man than I, that's for sure."

"I'm not sure *brave* is the word I would use."

Something in Liselle's tone drew Gerard's eye back to her face. She stood in profile to him, and though her full lips still smiled, an undeniable line of tension pulled at her mouth and strained along her jaw. Gerard frowned. He'd known Lady Liselle for many years at the king's court in Telianor. He'd seen her go through dalliances with carefree abandon, both before her marriage and following her widowhood. Years ago, he'd watched her make a valiant play for Terryn's affections, and for a little while there, he rather thought she'd win. He'd never been entirely certain what had transpired between them. Terryn wasn't a man to speak willingly—or at all—concerning matters of the heart.

But Liselle gave her head a little shake and turned to Gerard. "I have a message for you," she said, her voice once more as bright as the gleaming chandeliers above. "Your lovely bride has found the room too warm and crowded for her tastes and has ventured out to the lake walk. She bade me ask you to join her."

"Really?" Gerard's gaze locked once more with Liselle's. He knew he betrayed himself in that moment, knew that she sensed the sudden surging of his heart. Liselle's brows drew together ever so slightly, and Gerard hastily dropped his gaze. Liselle was Cerine's lady, yes, but she had been Fayline's lady first. And her dearest friend. "I . . . thank you for the message," he said, giving her a quick nod.

Liselle, one brow slightly upraised, sank into a deep curtsy as he brushed past her. Gerard hurried along the periphery of the room, making his way to the doors. People tried to stop and speak to him as he passed, and he was obliged to pause and press hands and smile and speak glib pleasantries every few paces, until he thought he might go mad.

He was just nearing the exit when a solid figure stepped into his way.

"Uncle. Well met," Gerard said through a gritted smile. "If you'll excuse me—"

Fendrel put out a hand and caught Gerard by the shoulder. He was possibly the only man in the room who would physically stop the prince in his tracks. Gerard's eyes flashed, and it was all he could do to keep from smacking his uncle's hand away.

When he met Fendrel's gaze, he hesitated. Fendrel looked like a man who'd just seen a glimpse of his own death.

"Gerard," the dominus said, his voice very low, almost impossible to hear over the flying dance music, "what is the nature of Terryn's relationship to this Venatrix di Ferosa?"

"What? Terryn and Ayleth?" Gerard looked back over his shoulder to where his venator and venatrix whirled in a flourish of dance just as the song reached its crescendo. "They are . . . competitors," he said with an unconvincing shrug. "As far as I know, nothing more."

"Are you sure?"

Gerard turned back to his uncle, meeting those iron-hard eyes of his. "Why does it matter?" he asked. "If you're so concerned, ask Terryn yourself."

Fendrel's fingers tightened their hold. He took a step nearer to his nephew, and when he spoke, his voice was a growl. "We've worked too hard for your future, Gerard," he said. "Don't throw it all away. Do you hear me? You don't know what all we've done to put you on this path."

A cold shadow fell across Gerard's soul. He saw again, in a brief flash behind his eyes, Cerine's face upraised to his, her lips forming words she hardly dared speak: "*Do you see? Do you understand?*"

He did understand. He'd known all along that he wasn't who they told him he was. He'd known all along his life was a lie.

But he knew as well that it was a lie he could never escape.

Gerard caught hold of Fendrel's wrist and wrested it from his shoulder with a vicious tug. "I think I do know," he answered, his lip curling. "Don't worry, Uncle. I'm still your Haunts-damned Golden Prince."

Startled by the venom in Gerard's voice, Fendrel

blinked and drew back a step. Gerard took the chance opportunity to dodge past his uncle and slip through the ballroom's outer doors into the candlelit passage beyond.

For several paces he couldn't recall why he had made this escape, so hot was the blood boiling in his veins. He wanted to . . . he wasn't sure what. He wanted to smash his fist into the castle wall and bring all of Dunloch crumbling down. Crumbling down on the heads of his father, his uncle, Duke d'Aldreda . . . all these people who had taken hold of his life and ground it into their preconceived molds, ground him so viciously that he couldn't begin to guess who he might be without their work. Even Terryn, whom he trusted more than anyone else in the world, refused to see him as anything other than the Golden Prince. Was there anyone in this world who could look at him and see the truth?

"Cerine."

Her name slipped from his lips almost unconsciously. He lifted his head, squared his shoulders, and hurried on down the passage, making for the open back doors leading out to the gardens and the lake walk.

Cerine was the only one who knew him. Who truly

*knew* him. Better than Terryn did. Certainly better than Fayline ever had. Cerine saw through the artifice, saw through the veils, and she knew Gerard du Glaive, the man, not the prince.

But could she ever love him? Knowing what she knew?

Wind gusted down the passage, and Gerard hastened into it, relieved to feel that cool touch on his flushed face. The moon was high and still strangely red in the sky above as he emerged onto the stone-paved patio and hurried across the greensward to the rippling lakeshore. His gaze scanned down below along the walkway at the water's edge, but he didn't see Cerine just yet. Perhaps she'd gone around to the west side of the north towers, beyond his sight.

He hurried down the steps, his heart pounding with eagerness. The strains of music from the ball faded, and the world around him was quiet that cold night. Was it possible Cerine truly wanted his company? The night of their wedding. In a few short hours, they would be led away to his rooms, and he would be expected to perform his duty as prince, as heir, ensuring the continuation of the line of the Chosen King. And Cerine, he did not doubt, would submit meekly to the will that had forced her into this position.

Gerard ground his teeth hard, his jaw aching. He couldn't do that to her. He wouldn't. Legacies be damned to the Haunts, he wouldn't make Cerine into some sort of useful object. He wouldn't treat her as his mother had been treated, forcing her to produce sons who existed only to serve the purpose established by others.

But what if she answered those questions he'd asked her in that foolish, foolish letter of his? What if she answered, and her answer mirrored what he had sometimes believed he'd glimpsed in her eyes? What if . . . what if . . .?

He dared not finish the thought.

He hastened along the lake walk, his eyes searching in the moonlight for some glimpse of her gold-trimmed gown. "Cerine?" he called softly.

"Gerard, my love."

Gerard stopped dead in his tracks. His heart dropped, and his knees turned to water. He seemed to have forgotten how to breathe.

He knew that voice. He *knew that voice.*

A figure approached along the walkway. She passed through the deep shadows cast by the retaining wall and stepped into a patch of moonlight, which glowed bright upon a lovely face framed in a mass of golden curls.

"My darling, at last! Do you know me?" Fayline said, speaking through Lady Liselle's mouth.

# CHAPTER 17

TERRYN DUCKED OUT OF THE BALLROOM TO CATCH his breath. He couldn't step away for long; officially speaking, he was on duty. Under orders from his Venator Dominus to keep an eye on Venatrix di Ferosa through-out the night's festivities.

But if he kept an eye on her for one moment more without some sort of reprieve, he was going to lose his mind.

So, he slipped away from the candlelight and music

into the quieter shadows of the empty great hall for a chance to catch his breath. Hidden inside his dress uniform were all manner of poisoned darts, and he even wore a decorative but fully functional scorpiona on a holster at his thigh. He busied himself checking the scorpiona now, sliding it from its holster and turning it round in his hands, determined to focus his attention on anything but the memory of Ayleth's shining eyes, of her hand lightly touching his. Of those scars only faintly hidden beneath layers of cosmetics, trailing across her collarbones and down between her pale breasts . . .

His face burned, and he concentrated hard on the scorpiona, his movements brisk and businesslike as he tested the firing mechanism, the tightness of the bowstring, the fastenings attaching it to the ornamental bracer. When there was nothing left to pretend to check, he holstered it and moved on to counting the darts tucked away on his person, then closed his eyes and reached inside, testing the strength of the Suppression spell he'd used on his shade. A complex spell, one that kept the spirit deeply subdued but was held in place by a single thread of magic, which he could snap if necessary, drawing power at moment's notice if need arrived. All was as it should be, and—

Her face, flushed with triumph, flashed before his mind's eye.

Wincing, Terryn focused on his scorpiona once more, pulled it from its holster, and held it up for closer inspection. Though his eyes fixed intently upon the intricacies of the weapon, his attention was too far gone elsewhere. He saw again the way her skirts hung about her hips, not suspended by structured undergarments but wafting close to her womanly figure. He saw again the way her bare shoulders moved in sensuous rhythm as the music filled her soul. He recalled how she had felt in his arms the night before, when she shoved him up against the granary wall, her hands against his chest, her face so close to his own. His gut churned with a growing fire that was both intoxicating and excruciating.

One hand clenched into a fist, Terryn rapped his forehead. He must master himself, master these feelings. He was better than this! A true Evanderian, devoted to the teachings of the saint. Yes, he'd suffered his share of carnal temptations—memory of Lady Liselle's soft lips and willing curves had plagued him off and on over the years. How she had pushed him, teased him, weakened him, trying to break through the resolve of his holy vows!

But he had triumphed in the end. And over the years, thoughts of Liselle had faded. Using the heat that had once burned with such agony inside him, he'd refined a will of iron. Nevermore would he allow himself to dance so close to the precipice of sin. The fire of the mortal flesh could not vanquish the sacred fire of a soul wholly devoted to the Goddess's service.

Until now.

He had to get her out of his head. Before this went any further. She was his opponent. His enemy. She stood in his way, both on his path to true holiness and on his road to success. He needed to . . . he needed to . . .

He needed to kiss her before the volcano inside him erupted.

"Venator."

It was the last voice he wanted to hear at that moment.

"Haunts damn it!" he hissed. But he turned and offered a crisp salute. "Dominus," he said, chin high, face masked in attention.

Thunder gathered on Fendrel's brow as he strode across the floor, the click of his boot heels echoing off the walls. Shadow-light flared in his eyes, and Terryn realized that the dominus's shade was straining against its song bindings. This was unlike the Fendrel Terryn knew, who ordinarily kept his shade in perfect order. But the Fendrel Terryn knew had never needed to wear three iron spikes on his left arm.

Fendrel crossed to Terryn, snarling as he came, "What do you think you are doing?"

"Sir?" Terryn gazed blandly into the space over his former master's shoulder.

"Don't play the fool." Fendrel caught Terryn by the arm and dragged him down the nearest passage, making for the quieter parts of the castle, farther from the ball. Instinct jumped in Terryn's muscles, and he very nearly threw the older man's hand off. But he maintained his composure, respecting his superior, until Fendrel hauled him into the long gallery of portraits and roughly pushed him a few paces away. Terryn drew himself upright, resuming his attentive stance, his hands behind his back.

"You cannot dance with that girl," Fendrel said. He

paced back and forth like a caged animal.

Terryn cleared his throat. "Did you or did you not command me to escort her and keep an eye on her throughout the evening?"

Fendrel's eyes flashed. "Don't throw my words back at me, boy. I said *watch* her, not fawn over her like a lovesick fool."

A cold shard of ice slid down Terryn's spine. He drew himself up straighter than ever.

"I will see to it that she is removed from this borough," Fendrel continued. "I will put this ridiculous competition to an end. But in the meantime, you must avoid her. At all costs. No more of this"—he waved a furious, vague hand—"whatever it was that I witnessed just now. You must remember who you are; you must remember where you are going. You must remember the plans I have for you. I don't want you dragged before the Council, accused of bedding your own hunt sister. They'll demand your head for it, and no power in this world will save you then, either your body or your soul."

Terryn's gaze fixed on the nearest of the portraits hung on the wall across from him—the image of Queen

Leurona, her infant prince seated on her lap. Her cold blue eyes gazed into Terryn's like a mirror image.

"Well?" Fendrel planted himself in Terryn's line of sight, cutting off his view of the queen. "What have you to say for yourself?"

Terryn waited a breath before speaking. But he had to know. "Who is she?"

Fendrel's nostrils flared, and the shadow-light sparked in his eyes.

"Who is she?" Terryn persisted. "You know her. You've met her before. But how or why or when or where, I cannot guess. I've known you for as long as I can remember, Fendrel. I've served at your side most of my life, but I don't know how you and she are connected."

"It doesn't matter." Fendrel's voice was harsh in his throat.

"It *does* matter." Terryn squeezed his left wrist tight, struggling to hold his temper in check. "Because from where I'm standing, Ayleth, Venatrix di Ferosa, has twice saved the future Queen of Perrinion from a witch. The very witch who managed to thwart you time and again. She has proven herself true to the Order, throwing herself into the very jaws of death for the sake of those she serves. And it's not just this time, Fendrel; I've seen her do it over and over again."

Fendrel turned away, his shoulders hunching. A dangerous aura oozed from the center of his spirit, strong enough to make Terryn hesitate. But Terryn was too angry now. He continued, regardless.

"Is she the most skillful, the best-trained venatrix? Hardly. But she is the most devoted to the protection of her borough of anyone I have ever met. Saint Evander himself could not find fault with her courage, with her passion, and yet you—*you*, Fendrel—seem to look at her as some sort of devil. And why? Is it just because she stands in my way?" With these words, Terryn planted himself in front of Fendrel, trying to force the man to meet his gaze. "Is that how little you think of me?"

Fendrel did not turn away, but he averted his eyes, glancing off to one side rather than look at Terryn.

"Is that how little you think of my abilities?" Terryn persisted, each word strained with anger so that his deep voice threatened to break. "Do you doubt I can prove myself worthy of Wodechran in Gerard's eyes? Do you doubt I can take Milisendis on my own merit? Then let me tell you something: I doubt it too. Because I cannot begin to hurl myself into each hunt with half the passion I see in Venatrix Ayleth!"

"That's quite the ardent speech coming from you," Fendrel rumbled. But there was something strange in his voice now. Not the rage Terryn had sensed before. Something else. Some powerful emotion that didn't make sense. Something like . . . like sorrow. It disturbed Terryn, and he drew back a pace, folding his arms defensively.

Fendrel sighed and rubbed a hand down his face. "I knew a venatrix once," he said, "who fought as fiercely as you have just described. She would give her life in a heartbeat for the sake of another. But such passion as that . . . it's dangerous, Terryn. It can lead to the downfall of kingdoms if it goes unchecked."

Terryn frowned. "Fendrel," he said, "you need to tell me the truth. Who is Ayleth that you should fear her?"

"I don't fear her." Fendrel's head came up, and the shadow-light flashed again. "I'll never fear her or any of her kind. I have ground them all beneath my heel, and I will grind her as well. Because, Terryn, that girl, that creature you were just dancing with, she is . . ."

His voice trailed off. His eyes widened. Terryn, hanging on that silence, waiting with his heart in his throat for the next words his former master would speak, nearly reached out and caught the dominus by his jerkin, nearly shook him until his bones rattled. But Fendrel turned away, looked back along the gallery.

"Did you hear that?" he said.

Terryn tilted his head. He heard nothing, not with his mortal ears. But reaching tentatively inside, beneath the humming Suppression song, he accessed his shade's senses and cast them out searchingly.

A scream. A woman's scream. A voice Terryn recognized at once.

"Fayline," he breathed.

He was in motion first, but Fendrel was only a split second behind. They pounded down the gallery, out into the passage, and raced down the garland-strewn hall for the back doors. As they burst out into the open night air, another scream assaulted their senses, both shade and mortal.

Then Gerard's voice cried out, "Away from me! Get

away!"

"Don't you see me? Don't you know me? Say my name! Say my name, my love!"

Terryn nearly fell down the steps to the lake walk in his haste, and only Fendrel's hand catching his elbow stopped him from careening into the water itself. They both skidded and turned, coming within sight of the scene taking place.

Liselle, collapsed in a pile of skirts at Gerard's feet, tore at her hair, tore at her face until blood streamed from long cuts and stained her nails. "It's me, Gerard! It's me! I've come back for you. Have you any idea what I have suffered to be with you again? Do you know the horrors I've seen?"

"You can't be her," Gerard answered. One of her hands caught his, and he struggled desperately to pull himself free. "She's dead. She's gone. Gone to the Haunts."

"Oh, I've been to the Haunts." The voice coming from Liselle's mouth went dark and dreadful, hardly human, yet it still recognizably belonged to Fayline. And from the center of her soul blazed the brilliance of an

Evanescer shade, almost blinding in its potency. "I've experienced that hell. And I'll never return, I tell you! But I can't live in this world without you, Gerard. You must come with me now. I'll take you away with me. We're still married to one another, remember? Those vows you spoke tonight are nothing but words, for our vows still stand! But we'll go away together, even as we were always meant to—"

"Unhand him, Inren!"

Fendrel's voice roared across the night. The shade-taken turned with a hiss, and Fendrel's dart whirred through the air. She vanished—and the dart soared out into the water. But Fendrel's shout had served its purpose, for she had let go of the prince before evanescing.

Terryn reached into the secret fold of his dress uniform, pulling out the Gentle Death. He did not have an Evanescer poison on him, for that shade was supposed to be gone. Ayleth herself had told him she'd seen it swallowed up in the Haunts. Had she lied to him? Or simply misunderstood what she saw?

"Get down!" Fendrel shouted, catching Terryn by the

arm and pulling him just as a bolt of blackness burst in the air where he had been. Liselle stepped through, her eyes blazing with magic and malice, her laughing mouth twisted into a hideous leer. With an inhuman shriek, she lunged at Fendrel. He knocked away her left hand, but her right caught hold of his shirt.

"Come with me, Venator," she said.

Fendrel gasped.

*"No!"* Terryn shouted and lashed out at the shade-taken. But another blast of blackness knocked him off his feet. Liselle and Fendrel vanished into the Haunts.

# CHAPTER 18

THE KING WAS WATCHING HER AGAIN. NOWHERE IN the crowded ballroom seemed to be safe from his eye.

Ayleth managed to secure a glass of something cool from the refreshment table and dart back behind her potted tree, but every time she peered out from the screen of its beribboned branches, she found herself meeting Guardin's gaze. He sat tall in his thronelike chair on the dais, his hands resting on its arms, his attitude relaxed. Yet there was a knife of tension in his eyes, betraying his true state of mind. Though her shade was suppressed, Ayleth didn't need Laranta's senses to feel the battlefield energy emanating from Guardin's soul. Energy that focused on her every move.

Should she be flattered? Possibly . . . if she could make herself believe the Chosen King's fixation with her was due to her heroism or even her beauty. But she couldn't shake the memory of that horror-filled flash in his eye when she'd bowed before him just the day before.

She retreated behind the tree again. How long was she expected to stay at this ball, anyway? She took another sip from her glass and peered out through the leaves, scanning the crowds and mentally planning her route of escape. If her eye strayed in search of a certain tall figure in a red sash, she pulled it quickly back under control. What did she care where Venator Terryn had gone off to? Or Lady Liselle either, for that matter. They were no doubt secreted away together in some hidden corner of the garden, or . . .

Ayleth shook her head sharply and took a step back further behind her screen of greenery. Her foot trod on a skirt, her own . . . or so she thought until she heard someone else gasp.

"Haunts!" Ayleth hissed, and whirled about to find herself staring into Lady Cerine's enormous eyes behind their thin veil.

Cerine blinked quickly. "I'm so sorry! I didn't realize anyone was back here. I . . . I was just trying to . . ."

"Hide?"

The lady pressed her lips into a thin smile and shrugged. "Perhaps."

Ayleth pulled aside a swath of her bountiful skirts to make space for Cerine's. "There's plenty of room. Besides, I'm plotting my getaway."

"Not one for dances, are you, Venatrix?"

"Um. No." Ayleth gave Cerine a look. "Neither are you, I gather."

This time the lady flashed a real smile, however brief. "No. I miss my scriptorium, to be honest. I was training to be a scribe, before . . ." She waved a hand vaguely out at the noble company, the lights, the display of wealth, the music. "Before all this."

Remembering the novice she'd met in the ruins of Cró Ular, Ayleth nodded. Despite her best efforts, she realized that she liked Lady Cerine d'Aldreda. She'd had every intention of disliking whoever was trussed up in a crown and jewels to marry the Golden Prince. No one, she'd believed, could ever be his equal. But this girl was more than a pretty doll draped in diamonds and silks. Memories of her last fight with the Phantomwitch were faint and confused, but Ayleth retained one particularly vivid image of the shorn-haired novice standing over her with broken pieces of a chamber pot in her hands.

Cerine had pluck. More than that, she had real courage where it counted. No one would ever be Gerard's equal. But maybe . . . maybe this young woman could come close.

Uncertain what more she could say, Ayleth took a last sip from her glass and looked back out into the room. Daring a glance in the direction of the king's high seat, she shuddered to find his gaze on her once again. Goddess above, couldn't he forget about her for an instant? It was past time to leave.

She took the first step to dart out from the screening foliage, but before she took the second, Cerine caught her elbow. "I'm sorry, Venatrix, but I have to ask . . . Have you seen the prince?"

In all her confusion and discomfort, Ayleth realized she'd lost track of Gerard's whereabouts. She turned now, scanning the crowd again, trying to ignore Guardin's constant stare. "I don't see—"

A scream sliced through the festive sounds of the ballroom. Ayleth nearly jumped out of her skin. Other voices screamed in response to the first, making the cacophony so overwhelming, Ayleth couldn't discern the source of terror.

The crowd on the dance floor scattered, falling over themselves in their desperation to flee. At the epicenter of their flight, a cloud of twining *oblivis* threads dissipated as it spread, revealing Lady Liselle . . . and, lying at her feet, Fendrel, his jerkin still gripped in her hand, his back arched painfully against her hold.

For one breath, Ayleth stood frozen, unable to believe her eyes. For a second breath, she realized that not only was her shade suppressed, but she had no weapons, no pipes— Haunts damn it, she didn't even have a pair of trousers!

On the third breath, she leapt into action.

Ignoring how the seams under her arms ripped, Ayleth lunged through the screaming revelers and threw herself at the refreshments table. She'd seen a suckling pig displayed on a silver platter, and she was fairly certain a carving knife had lain next to it. In her haste, she rammed into the table, knocking over balanced dishes and glasses and carafes of water and wine. There was the knife! She snatched it up by the blade, flicking it fast in the air and catching it by the hilt. Then she whirled to face the dance floor.

Everild was already there.

The older venatrix, clad in her dress uniform, took a firing stance on the far side of the room, aiming her scorpiona at Liselle's exposed back. Just as she took the shot, a fleeing lord jostled her elbow, and her aim went wide. The dart clattered and slid uselessly across the floor.

The shade-taken Liselle, seeing the dart, dropped her hold on Fendrel and spun to face Everild. A terrible smile tore across her face. Everild's eyes widened, and she spat a curse before lunging two steps forward just as the shade-taken vanished in another burst of darkness. Everild dropped to her knees, narrowly avoiding Liselle's grasping arms as she lurched out of the void behind her. The venatrix swung her left arm, the iron spike on her bracer whistling through the air. But she wasn't fast enough.

Liselle stepped out of the world and back in again, this time directly in front of Everild. She caught the venatrix by her short hair and slammed her face-first into the floor. Everild went limp like a doll.

Ayleth roared and took a step. Her foot caught in the folds of her Haunts-damned gown, and she fell heavily to her knees. The knife slipped from her fingers and slid, spinning across the floor, back behind the potted tree where she had taken refuge moments ago. Yanking herself up, tripping and stumbling, Ayleth struggled to reach her weapon even as another flurry of movement drew her eye back to the dance floor.

The guards who had stood so solemnly along the walls now flooded to the dais, twelve strong, all with weapons upraised in a bristling shield of sharp steel. King Guardin was already halfway down the steps, and he threw himself at the backs of the two guards standing in his way, shouting, "No! Let me through! My brother!"

His word as king was ineffective against his men. Though he struggled, three of them grabbed him by the arms and the back of his fine clothes, hauling him away and out through one of the tall windows, Guardin hurling curses and threats with every step.

It was a brave gesture on the part of those guardsmen. If the shade-taken had been interested in them or their master, they all could have been dragged to the Haunts within moments with no defense, nothing they could do to fight back. But the spirits inside Liselle spared no more than a passing glance for the king. Instead, a figure approaching the dance floor caught her attention, a figure wearing gaudy green-and-gold garments.

Duke d'Aldreda's face was paler than Ayleth had ever seen it, stark white beneath his red pompadour and embroidered eyepatch. He looked into the eyes of the shade-taken Liselle.

"Inren," he said. "They told me you were banished to the Haunts where you belong."

Liselle tilted her head fetchingly, tossing her golden hair like a child. "Oh, Father dearest, I'm not *her*. Do you really wish to see your eldest child Haunts-bound?"

The duke's one eye widened. "Fayline," he breathed. A light resembling hope filled his face, a light too warped with sorrow to be real, and he took a step toward her. "Fayline, is that really you?"

"Indeed. Not in the flesh, alas. My flesh was spoiled, ruined. And then you went and burned it. I had to find a new host, and dear Liselle's body presented itself just at the opportune moment. I'd seen to it that she still had one of the witch's anchors on her, so when our spirits were loosed, we were able to use the last of our strength to return to that anchor and claim the available body." She shrugged and lowered her eyes briefly. "Sadly, there was no room inside for poor Liselle. So, we ousted her."

"Not you," the duke said, though he drew back a little and his voice shook. "You would never oust the soul of your friend. Liselle was like a sister to you."

"Yes, well, sisters don't mean as much to me as they once did," the shade-taken snarled. "Speaking of which, where is that little chit in the bridal veils? She and I must have words."

The duke drew the decorative sword he wore from its sheath. It was a gilded, bejeweled thing, but its steel was true. He held it out steadily before him, his gaze firm. "You are not Fayline," he said in a voice so dreadful, it could break hearts. "She would never speak of her sister with such words. I know you, Inren. I was your slave too long not to recognize you."

*"I am not Inren!"* Liselle screamed. Then she pitched forward, as though she would throw herself heart-first onto the duke's blade. He lunged, his whole body extending into the thrust. But before the point of steel connected with her bare breast, the shade-taken stepped into the chaos of darkness.

The duke staggered, fell to one knee. His single eye lifted to meet Ayleth's across the room. He looked at her without recognition, blinking, his mouth agape.

Liselle reappeared behind him and caught him by the hair on top of his head. Gnashing her teeth so that blood and spittle flew, she plucked a knife hidden in the folds of her voluminous gown and plunged it into the duke's throat.

His cry cut off abruptly in a spurt of blood. Red spilled in brilliant stain over his perfectly cut jacket. He dropped his sword with a clatter, pressing both hands to the wound. Blood gushed through his jeweled fingers, an unstoppable fountain. His body writhed, and he choked, struggled, fell . . . and died.

A hideous shriek tore from Liselle's mouth, and she shook her head wildly, staring down at the broken body of d'Aldreda. "I didn't want to! I didn't want to, Father!" she cried. Then she smiled a lunatic's smile. "But Inren did, and oh! Oh, how happy she is!"

Ayleth, watching all this as though it took place in some distant world, shook herself hard. Enough. Her searching hand found the knife, and she stood upright. With a quick slash, she cut a long slit up the front of her silk gown. She was still trapped in the constricting corset, and she didn't have Laranta—but she wouldn't stand by a moment longer.

"Fayline!" she yelled.

The shade-taken's head turned sharply, and Liselle's lovely face contorted with fury. "Festering damn. I should have killed you by now."

Ayleth threw her knife. She didn't care in that moment whether she dealt a violent death. She put all the force of her arm into that throw, and the knife whistled through the air and cut the cloud of *oblivis* whirling where Liselle's eye had been an instant before.

Ayleth cursed and hurled herself to the floor, preparing for the shade-taken's reappearance beside her. What other weapon could she find? A broken dish knocked from the table caught her eye, and she scrambled toward it, thinking perhaps to use the sharp edge.

"Father?"

The quavering voice caught Ayleth's attention. Cerine stood in the doorway of the ballroom, her veil pulled from her face, her skin white as a ghost's. She'd been caught up in the crowd of people rushing in terror from the room but had fought her way back again. Her eyes fixed on the dead body lying in pooling blood.

"My lady, get out of here!" Ayleth shouted. The shade-taken could appear again at any moment.

But Cerine, deaf to Ayleth's cry, staggered across the polished floor where, mere minutes ago, dancers had twirled in delight. She threw herself on her knees beside d'Aldreda's body. "Father, Father!" she cried, catching hold of his shoulders. "Father, get up!"

The little fool. Did she not realize the danger she was

in? Ayleth snatched up her bit of broken plate and scrambled to her feet, ready to rush at Cerine and drag her bodily from the room. But where could she take her? Where would she be safe when the shade-taken could appear anywhere, at any moment?

A pounding of footsteps, and she turned to see Gerard in the doorway, out of breath, his hair falling in his face. Terryn arrived two steps behind the prince, his scorpiona already up, his body assuming firing stance.

"Cerine!" Gerard cried, then stopped in his tracks, taking in the fallen bodies—Fendrel, Everild, the duke. Struck dumb, he could only stare.

Terryn, however, took in the situation in an instant. He caught Gerard by the back of the shirt, hauling him across the floor to a corner of the cavernous room. "Stand there!" he barked, bracing himself in a wide stance in front of the prince. "She can't appear behind you if your back is to the wall."

Ayleth immediately saw the wisdom of this maneuver. Gerard must have understood as well, for he retreated right up to the wall, pressing tight into the corner. Only his front remained accessible, and Terryn stood there as a human shield. "Cerine, come to me!" Gerard called to his betrothed.

Still weeping over her father's body, Cerine did not seem to hear him. Ayleth gripped her broken plate and started toward the girl, intending to pick her up and push her into that corner along with Gerard.

Terryn's voice arrested her mid-stride. "Venatrix, arm yourself!" he barked.

Ayleth turned and met his gaze, uncertain what he meant. His eyes swiveled to the fallen body of Everild, not far from where she stood. Of course!

Gathering her skirts up in both hands, Ayleth rushed to Everild's side and crouched beside her. When she rolled the venatrix onto her back, she gasped in surprise and relief to realize that Everild breathed. The woman's face was a mass of blood, her nose broken, but she was alive.

Fingers trembling, Ayleth unfastened the decorative but functional scorpiona on Everild's right arm, then reached for various quivers and poisons. Had the venatrix thought to bring an Evanescer poison with her? No, why would she? The only known Evanescer shade was presumably banished to the Haunts.

Ayleth grabbed the Gentle Death instead and rose, assuming a defensive position. Some instinct made her glance at the fallen venatrix one last time. The Vocos pipes in their sheath on Everild's belt caught her eyes, and her hand reached for the instrument.

Another bolt of darkness, just to her left.

Ayleth spun in a crouch, her fingers clutching the Vocos. She raised the scorpiona armed with the Gentle Death, but her actions were too quick, her aim not certain. The dart flew wide, missing the shade-taken Liselle by a foot or more, and crashed into a pillar.

The witch faced Terryn in the corner but looked past him to Gerard. "My love, do you hide from me?" she said, her voice breaking with tears. "Don't look at me like that, Gerard! Am I such a monster to you?"

"Don't answer her," Terryn snarled, taking a step back, leaving almost no space between himself and the prince. Gerard stared at Liselle over the venator's shoulder, his face stricken.

His eyes moved. And that which possessed Liselle's body followed his gaze and spied Cerine crouched over her father's body, frozen like a mouse under the cat's stare.

"No, no, no," Ayleth hissed, fumbling for another dart. Before she could get her weapon loaded, the shade-taken vanished again, and this time Ayleth knew exactly where she would reappear. She slammed the Gentle Death into the scorpiona and swung it around, pointing it into the empty space just behind Cerine, who sat upright, pulling away from her dead father, and started to scramble backwards.

The world tore open, and through the tear stepped the shade-taken Liselle in a cloud of *oblivis*. She had situated herself perfectly, angled so that Cerine's body served as a shield blocking any chance of a clear shot from Ayleth or Terryn. Cerine recognized her vulnerable position and flung herself forward, attempting to clear a shot for the venators. But Liselle snatched her by the arm and, twisting painfully, dragged her upright, pulling her against her chest.

"Move one finger, any of you, and she dies!"

Ayleth froze. Liselle's knife, still stained with d'Aldreda's blood, pointed at Cerine's throat.

"What do you say, sister mine?" Fayline's voice hissed through Liselle's smile even as she tickled the knife's point up and down Cerine's skin, along her jawline and down to her collarbone. "Would you like to take a journey to the Haunts? I could leave you there easily enough."

"Stop!"

Gerard's voice echoed across the room, drawing every eye to the corner where he stood. Terryn squared off, trying to make himself an impenetrable barrier between the prince and the shade-taken, but Gerard pushed around his venator's elbow, one hand outstretched.

"Fayline," he said, his voice soft and gentle. "Fayline, enough of this." His gaze flitted toward the dance floor where Duke d'Aldreda lay in his pooling blood, where Everild and Fendrel sprawled inert, but he quickly refocused his attention on the shade-taken. "Fayline, this isn't your doing. I know it isn't. You're not vicious; you're not cruel."

The shade-taken Liselle wrenched harder on Cerine's arm, and the girl whimpered. "You don't know what I am," Fayline said through Liselle's mouth. "You don't know what I've had to become. All so that I could return to you! But what do I find upon returning?" She pressed the edge of her blade harder, and blood trickled down Cerine's white skin, pooling in the hollow of her collarbone.

"Stop, please," Gerard said, his voice only quavering slightly. Though Terryn reached out one arm, trying to restrain him, he shook his head and forced his way past the venator. Taking three careful steps, he never broke gaze with the shade-taken. "My . . . my darling, let her go. She doesn't deserve—"

"Doesn't deserve what? To die?" The shade-taken laughed horribly but pulled the blade away from Cerine's throat to wave it in a sweeping gesture. "This traitorous little whore who stole you from me? While I was suffering in the darkness of the Witchwood, while my own body betrayed me, while my soul was pummeled and tortured and nearly driven out into the dark, *she* stepped in and wooed you with her sly words and her poisonous innocence. She couldn't wait until I was gone so she could make her play! And you dare stand there and tell me she doesn't deserve everything I can give her?"

"She doesn't matter." Gerard shook his head slowly. The muscle under his eye twitched, but his voice was steady. "The only one who matters is you, Fayline. You're the only one I've ever seen." He held his right hand out, turned palm upward, reaching for her as though asking for a dance. "Please, my love. Take me. Take me with you, and we'll go away together. You and I, like we were always meant to be. Leave Cerine and give me your hand. Give me your hand, Fayline."

Ayleth's eyes moved to Terryn. She saw how he focused, saw that if the shade-taken let go of Cerine even for a second, he would take his shot. She silently urged him to hold still, to not draw attention to himself.

But the shade-taken didn't move. She waited as Gerard drew nearer and nearer. Ayleth wanted to scream, wanted to warn him not to get any closer! His back was now directly blocking Terryn's line of sight, and Terryn would have to shift his position to take the shot—which would immediately remind the shade-taken of his presence.

"What an interesting tableau."

The shock of a new voice speaking into the tension nearly ripped a scream from Ayleth's lips. Though she hated to tear her gaze from the shade-taken Liselle, she turned, looking to the shadows of the dais, where a bowed, withered figure emerged, trailing glorious golden robes.

The old Grand Mother smiled as though bestowing a blessing upon all those gathered. "It seems we are at an impasse here, my dears," she said.

# CHAPTER 19

"WHO ARE YOU?" FAYLINE DEMANDED, SNEERING through Liselle's face at the old woman. She drew Cerine back against her more tightly than before. "Do I know you?"

The old priestess moved out from the shadows into the golden light of the chandeliers. Her flabby neck seemed to quiver in its effort to support the ornate headdress perched atop her head, and her scrawny arms were weighed down by the golden embroidery of her robes. When she was younger and stronger, she must have been an awe-inspiring sight, but now there was something grotesque about her fat, tottering figure swathed in such gorgeous raiment.

She drew herself up tall. Ayleth's sensitive ears heard a gasp, and she glanced back at Terryn. His firing arm lowered, and blood drained from his face, leaving him deathly pale.

"Ah," the priestess said, cackling delightedly. "The venator knows me. But then again, he should . . . my sweet little pet of days gone by."

"Ylaire," Terryn said, and swung his scorpiona back into position, sighting along its length. "Rot in hell!" But he didn't take the shot. He stood as though frozen, his arm tensed, every muscle straining, his eyes bugging from his skull.

The old priestess stood across from him, her arm upraised, her fingers tensed. And though Laranta was still suppressed inside Ayleth beneath the song spells, she could almost, *almost* sense the pulsing power of curse threads. The priestess was a shade-taken.

"Ylaire," Ayleth whispered in echo of Terryn. Like a

thunderclap, recognition struck: the Warpwitch.

She did not stop to think about her next move. She acted all in a breath, in that last breath she had before the Warpwitch turned on her. Ramming the Vocos into her mouth, she blew as hard as she could—one single, short, horrible, piercing note.

The sound shattered through her senses, screeching through every head in that room. The Warpwitch, Fayline, Cerine, Gerard—shade-taken or un-taken, they all screamed and pulled away from that blast like slicing knives through the ears. Only Terryn remained frozen where he stood, unable to react.

Ayleth dropped the pipes, her arms flinging wide, her head thrown back, her eyes staring straight up at the ceiling but seeing nothing. Nothing but the wild whirling of sheer power inside her head.

Laranta rose. Magic coursed just beneath Ayleth's skin, first warm, then hot, then searing. A maelstrom of otherworldly force and brilliance and pain burst through every vein of her body, surged through every hair, every molecule. What a fool she was to think she could control this! What a fool she was to imagine she would be safe!

Her soul would surely tear loose from her body and fly off like a flag ripped from its pole in a hurricane gale.

Laranta poured out of Ayleth's head and manifested before her on the ballroom floor, as large as a horse, her eyes like burning coals, her fangs flashing. The shade turned her enormous head and looked Ayleth directly in the eye.

*What need, Mistress?* she growled.

Ayleth fell to her knees, hardly able to bear the weight of power inside her. Yet, she realized, her soul remained ascendant. All Laranta's might and main flowed through her, but it was still hers to command.

*What need?* Laranta asked again, snarling in her bloodthirsty eagerness.

"*The Warpwitch!*" Ayleth cried, both in her head and with her mortal mouth. "*Stop the Warpwitch!*"

Laranta turned to focus her burning gaze on the old priestess's shivering form. With her shade's power ablaze in her head, flaming throughout her body, Ayleth saw the terrible shape of the spirit ascendant within that withered host. A hideous Anathema twined with the soul of the witch, a writhing, bloody, snake-like thing.

The witch screamed, lashing the air with one gnarled hand. A bolt of Anathema curse shot out from the spirit in her core, speeding straight for Laranta. It struck the wolf shade hard, and Laranta staggered under the blow. Pain rippled back along their shared soul tether, knocking Ayleth from her feet as if the bolt had been aimed directly at her.

Ayleth was up again in an instant. "*To me, Laranta!*" she cried, and flung herself directly at the old woman.

The Warpwitch threw out one hand to fend her off, but the curse she cast next wasn't aimed at Ayleth. Instead, she sent a bolt of magic careening along a different thread. "*Kill the prince!*" the Warpwitch shrieked.

Although Laranta's power surged inside her, urging her to throw herself into the witch, to tear the old woman apart with her bare hands, Ayleth stopped, turned. Her eyes widened.

A curse thread sharp as a razor plunged directly into Terryn's soul, anchored by the blazing sigil beneath the scar on his face. The sigil's blinding red light scorched through his skin, but this agony was nothing compared to the curse itself piercing to his very core. A command, a compulsion which he could not disobey.

Yet something inside him resisted. And his soul began to rip in two.

Terryn screamed. It was an utterly inhuman sound. He fell to his knees, fell to his hands, to his elbows, still screaming, his head curling in on his chest.

"Terryn!" Gerard cried, and took a step toward him.

"Stand back!" Terryn gnashed through teeth that were suddenly sharp, tearing into his own lips. His spine bent, buckled, and sharp protrusions of bone broke through his uniform.

Horror churned through Ayleth's soul. She knew this curse. She'd seen it before, and she knew what was happening. Terryn was becoming a monster.

Ayleth bared her teeth, turning back to fix the Warpwitch with the force of her stare. "Let him *go!*" she cried, and sprang across the ballroom. Laranta's overwhelming power coursed through her so that her feet barely touched the floor, and her hands reached out to catch the witch by her throat. One instant. That's all she needed—one instant, and she would break the host body's neck, and Goddess save them all from the spirits unleashed in violence!

Just before her fingers closed around the witch's old throat, a burst of darkness appeared on her right. A dainty white hand reached out from that darkness and caught her by the wrist.

"Don't touch her!" an unknown voice roared from Liselle's mouth.

Ayleth twisted her arm sharply, using Laranta's strength to break the shade-taken's hold. She ducked in time to avoid being caught by the other hand, and the shade-taken Liselle vanished. Knowing she had mere moments before the Evanescer reappeared, Ayleth lunged again at the Warpwitch. But the shade-taken priestess had already darted away and was twisting at the curse thread binding Terryn. Though her body was frail, the spirits inside it were potent and cruel.

Terryn screamed again, then rose up taller than his human height, a monster looming and growing, his limbs misshapen, spines bursting from his back, his shoulders, his neck.

"*The prince!*" shouted the Warpwitch, yanking on that curse thread as though pulling the leash of a pet. "*Kill the prince!"*

Terryn's head turned—heavy, mutated, his jaw open to expose hideous long teeth—and his glowing eyes fixed upon Gerard. The prince backed away one step, two. He was unarmed, not that any weapon could save him against such a power. He held up both hands.

"Terryn," he said. "Terryn, you know me—"

Ayleth leaped. Laranta's strength blazed in her limbs, propelling her across the ballroom to wrap her arms around Gerard's midsection, knock him off his feet, and carry him several yards away. Safely away from the explosion of pure white energy that streamed from Terryn's throat, breaking and melting the floor where it struck in a blast of deadly force.

Ayleth's back hit the wall, her arms around Gerard, her body shielding him from the impact. They sprawled where they landed, both scrambling to get their feet back under them. "What's happened to him?" Gerard cried.

Ayleth had no time to answer. The ends of her loose hair singed and sizzled from the heat of that blast. Terryn remained standing, still pouring every ounce of destructive power into that single blast at the floor, not yet realizing that his prey had escaped. She looked at him, illuminated in his own lethal blaze, and could hardly recognize Terryn anymore. He had become a monster, some creature from before the dawn of civilization, crushed unnaturally into a man's shape. And within that physical form she saw the pulsing of his Arcane shade as it struggled against its bindings, fighting the control of the Warpwitch's curse.

In a flash, she realized what must be done.

With a wild yell, she threw herself at that spiny back. Laranta flew with her as both a wolfish shadow at her side and a potent spirit within her. Ayleth caught hold of a spine protruding from the base of Terryn's skull and wrapped her arm around his thickened, scale-covered throat.

"Terryn!" she screamed, hoping against hope that he could hear her through the roaring pain and throbbing curse. "Terryn, let your shade go! It will help you! It will stop this!"

His long, misshapen arm swung back, trying to catch her, to pluck her off his back. She quickly swung to the other side, just avoiding his reach, and readjusted her grip around his neck. His body was hot, meltingly hot, and the sharp scales bursting through his skin cut into her exposed bosom and shoulders. She bared her teeth and held on tighter.

"Let go, Terryn!" she yelled again. "Loose your shade!"

"No!" he shouted, his voice warped and hideous, a roar of agony through his fangs. He tore at her again. This time his hand caught hold of her arm and dragged her off his back.

But she had Laranta's full strength inside her now. Catching hold of his arm, she pressed everything she had into his elbow, pushing against its natural bend. He might be mutated into a hellish fiend, but his body still responded to pain.

He shrieked, and another blast of energy shot from his mouth, narrowly missing her face. It struck the chair up on the dais, shattering it into a million pieces. She caught him by the throat, clamping his jaw shut. Her fingers pressed tight, and she poured Laranta's power into her grip, refusing to let him open his mouth again, refusing to let another blast escape. But she saw the writhing hot magic build up in his eyes. It would burst out of him one way or another—it would tear his body apart.

"Terryn!" she screamed. "Please!"

He blinked. For an instant, she thought she saw a flash of blue, thought she saw a glimpse of recognition.

Then his whole body jerked, every muscle spasming. He staggered to one side, dragging her with him, and fell heavily to one knee. One spine-grown hand caught at her skirts, but she broke its hold with ease, and he collapsed, sprawling on his stomach with limbs outspread.

A dart quivered in the back of his neck.

Ayleth followed the dart's trajectory back to its source: Fendrel du Glaive, propped up on one elbow, his face pale and drawn. His scorpiona arm was still upraised, shivering with the effort needed to hold it steady. Their eyes met for a moment.

Then the Venator Dominus groaned and bowed his head to the floor, unable to support its weight any longer.

Ayleth stepped back from the fallen Terryn. The Arcane poison would subdue him for hours yet; he was no longer a direct threat to the prince. She spun quickly, checking to make certain Gerard still stood by the wall where she'd left him. He stared at her, his mouth open, his skin glistening with sweat, his chest heaving as he gasped for breath. But he was alive and unharmed. Now for . . .

Ayleth turned in place, her gaze darting across the ballroom. *"Laranta? Laranta!"* she cried inside her head. *"Laranta, where are the shade-taken? Where are the witches?"*

Laranta's massive form leapt into her view, running to cover every inch of the floor, her nose twitching, her eyes burning. But Ayleth could sense the truth even without her shade's perceptions. The Warpwitch and the Phantomwitch were gone.

And so was Cerine.

# CHAPTER 20

WHAT COULD SHE DO? AYLETH STOOD DUMBSTRUCK, staring around the room. Shadow-light sparked in her eyes. What could she do? What could she try?

Sensing Ayleth's frantic questions, Laranta redoubled her efforts, rushing to each swirling patch of deadness where the shade-taken Liselle had stepped into and out from the Haunts, plunging her wolf nose into the poisonous tendrils, searching for some scent she might follow.

But there was nothing. The Phantomwitch had *evanesced*, taking both Ylaire and Cerine with her. Leaving no trail.

The urgency of the hunt beat in Ayleth's spirit without release. When she whimpered, the sound rippled along the tightly strung soul-tether connecting her to Laranta, and her shade whimpered as well, impotent and frustrated.

"Terryn!"

The frantic voice broke through the throbbing haze in her head. Ayleth pivoted, her ruined ballgown fluttering like the petals of a shredded rose. Gerard knelt at his friend's side; his hand reached for the Arcane dart.

"Stop!" Ayleth sprang across the distance and caught Gerard's wrist, yanking his arm back.

"Is it . . . is it the Gentle Death?" Gerard demanded, looking up at her with eyes so full of horror, she almost couldn't meet his gaze.

Ayleth shook her head. "It's a paralysis, nothing more. It will suppress his shade and give him time to recover."

Gerard dropped his gaze to the warped body of his friend. Already the terrible spines protruding from

Terryn's back began to retract and fade, leaving nothing but holes in his garments. The hand extended near her on the floor was still twisted in pain, but it was a human hand, no longer the savage claws of some primitive beast.

"What happened to him?" Gerard asked.

Before Ayleth could attempt an answer, movement caught her eye. Her instincts still on edge, she spun about. Laranta growled and leapt to her side, massive and threatening. But even Laranta flinched at the sight of Fendrel drawing himself upright, swaying on his feet, and bracing his legs apart. His shade roiled violently in his soul, warping Ayleth's vision so dramatically that she had to struggle to use her mortal eyes and see the human man beneath the spirit substance.

His shade, that strange, writhing wraith, was fighting for ascendancy.

Ayleth's hand went to her breast but discovered far too much bare skin and a roughly used gown rather than the quivers of poisons she had expected to find. Her gaze shot to the inert Everild, calculating the distance, wondering whether the older venatrix had an Anathema dart on her that might possibly be strong enough to suppress the mounting force of the shade in Dominus Fendrel.

She was just pulling herself together to make a leap when Fendrel unlatched the spring on his left arm bracer and the three iron spikes shot back, driving straight into his arm. A blast of pain radiated from his core—physical pain turned into spiritual torture. Ayleth's shadow sight perceived it as a dark shockwave of magic, and she threw up both arms as though to protect herself as it rolled outward from the dominus.

"Uncle, are you all right?" Gerard asked from his place beside Terryn. He could not perceive the battle between Fendrel's spirit and that of his shade. He saw only the use of the spikes and the red blood rolling down his uncle's arm from three small wounds.

Fendrel did not answer. The tendons in his throat stood out like cords as he fought to suppress a scream. But he did not fall, did not flinch. He let the waves of pain roll over him. Ayleth watched as his shade recoiled deeper and deeper, falling back under the suppressions until Fendrel was once more fully in control.

Only then did the dominus let the spikes spring back

on their hinges, a shuddering breath of relief slipping through his lips. He pressed a hand to the wounds, staunching the trickle of blood. On unsteady feet he took a step, then another, making his way to where Ayleth and the prince crouched over Terryn's fallen form.

Ayleth studied him hard as he approached. "How . . . how are you not *oblivis* infected?" she blurted. "She dragged you to the Haunts! How did you survive?"

Fendrel shook his head heavily and spoke through pain-tightened jaws. "I long ago established a curse I could use to latch hold of Inren, preventing her from doing to me what I've seen her do to so many of my brethren. She could not leave me in the Haunts, could not carry me there for more than an instant without risking her own safety."

It must be a powerful curse indeed, Ayleth thought. No wonder his shade had climbed so far ascendant. Fendrel must have dug deep to access that amount of raw power.

The dominus went down on one knee, released hold of his wounded left arm, and pressed two bloody fingers against Terryn's neck, feeling for a pulse. Satisfied, he then touched the ugly scar on Terryn's cheek, his face a study of stern concentration beneath the film of pain.

Ayleth knew without asking that the Warpwitch's curse on Terryn was not broken. With Laranta ascendant, she could see it, still alive and throbbing with magic, though currently subdued. It might be reawakened at any time.

"Can anything be done for him?" Ayleth asked.

Fendrel's eyes lifted to hers for a flashing instant. Then he stood, grabbing his wound again, and briefly rolled his neck. "Watch over him," he growled. "He will wake disoriented and in pain. Don't let him move too quickly or too soon."

This wasn't an answer to her question. However, it seemed to be the only answer she would get, since Fendrel turned and started toward the open ballroom door.

"Wait!" Gerard cried, leaping up to rush after his uncle. "We must find Cerine! They took her, Fayline and the priestess. The witches. They took Cerine. You've got to help me find her."

Fendrel placed his bloody right hand on Gerard's

shoulder and squeezed. "We will," he said. "We will do everything in our power to recover your bride. But now I must speak to your father. And you must get your house in order, Gerard. Find someone to care for Everild. See to your guests. Calm their fears if at all possible, but send them away from here without delay. Urge them not to speak of tonight's events, and squelch what rumors you can."

Gerard's face was stricken. He shook his head, then nodded, drawing a long breath. There was nothing else he could do. He knew as well as anyone that the Phantom-witch left no discernible trail.

Fendrel patted his nephew's shoulder again before turning once more to the door. He paused. As Ayleth watched, he unstrapped the iron-spiked bracer from his arm and, in a single fluid motion, pulled it free and tossed it straight to her. Ayleth caught it, deftly avoiding the sharp ends of the spikes still stained with Fendrel's shade-blighted blood. She met the dominus's eye.

"Use it," he said.

With that, he stepped through the doorway and vanished into the passage. Ayleth heard him shouting for the household guard, but her attention fixed on those spikes. Fendrel knew she had released Laranta's power. He could sense the ascendant power of her shade. Evander's law dictated the use of iron pain to suppress a fully ascendant shade.

It was ridiculous. There was no need to inflict such pain on herself or Laranta. Laranta would not overwhelm her, would never oust her soul from her body. Laranta . . .

She looked up, meeting the gaze of her wolf shade, which stood so huge and so brimming with magic only a few paces from her.

Laranta tilted her head to one side. *Mistress,* she said, *what need? What need?*

Ayleth grimaced. She could take Everild's Vocos again and play the Song of Suppression. She could use the suppressing spells easily enough, and she knew Laranta would obey.

But . . . did she know for certain? Laranta, in this ascendant state, could resist the songs and win. And once having tasted that strength, that supremacy, would she ever submit to Ayleth's control again?

Gerard watched her. She felt his gaze on the side of

her face, studying her, waiting to see if she would obey her dominus like a good venatrix. Using a fold of her skirt, she wiped Fendrel's blood from the spikes. Then slowly, methodically, she strapped the bracer to her left arm.

*Mistress,* Laranta said, taking several steps toward her. *Mistress, what will you do to me?*

Ayleth lifted tear-filled eyes, meeting her wolf shade's gaze. "*I'm sorry, Laranta,*" she said.

Then she flicked the mechanism and drove those three spikes down through flesh to the bone.

# CHAPTER 21

BODIES WERE FOUND. TOO MANY BODIES, HIDDEN away in unused rooms, stuffed under beds, heaped in empty stalls. Five were found before dawn, but more might still be discovered. One of them, tucked in an empty potato barrel in the kitchen cellar, was identified as a Siveline Sister, one of Mother Didienne's closest attendants.

*It happened again.*

In a haze of horror, Gerard spoke to his guard, spoke

to his chancellor, spoke to each of his guests in turn. He maintained a surface calm. He diminished the terror that had taken place, flatly refuted things he knew to be true, uttered promises he wouldn't remember in ten minutes' time . . . He preserved the peace, reestablished order. He provided physical, visual proof that the kingdom stood, that the power of his father's house remained firmly in place, that the will of the Goddess would prevail.

And all the while, drumming in the back of his head the thought: *It happened again. It will continue to happen. They will never be stopped. They will never be sated.*

Goddess's will be damned. The witches would tear apart the legacy of the Chosen King with their bare, bloody hands.

They would tear apart Cerine . . .

He dared not let himself think her name. All the false façade of strength he utilized to bolster himself would crumble away, leaving him weak and broken in the rubble.

The hours inched on, a never-ending succession of impossible tasks. The sun rose and climbed into the sky, and by the time it had reached its zenith, the pavilions that had dotted Dunloch's lawn were all torn down. The various parties of travelers and merrymakers hastened to leave behind the cursed walls of the castle on the holy lake. Only Duke d'Aldreda's entourage and the Siveline Sisters remained. Gerard had already turned over the duke's body to his people, but the Sisters . . . he could not face. How could he bear to tell them that their high priestess, their Grand Mother, had been taken by a shade? By a witch, no less.

At last, when he could stand no more, Gerard drove everyone out of his office and bade Chancellor Yves shut the door. For a few moments at least, he bowed his head, pressed the heels of his hands into his eyes, and concentrated on nothing more than drawing breath.

Faces appeared in the darkness behind his eyelids—Terryn, warped and monstrous with the ravages of a curse; Liselle, twisted with Fayline's heartbreak, spewing venom with every word she spoke; Fendrel, hard and dangerous with conviction underscored by abiding terror.

Cerine . . .

Cerine gazing at him across the room. Her arm twisted behind her, a knife at her throat.

"Goddess damn us all," Gerard hissed. This was his fault; he must face the truth before it crushed him under its weight. All of this was his fault: Cerine's kidnapping, Terryn's curse, d'Aldreda's death, Liselle's possession. Fayline's torment. If he had refused the duke's insistence that he take Cerine as his wife in Fayline's stead, none of this would have happened. But he'd been weak. So weak.

He rubbed his hands down his face, dashing away the single tear that escaped. It would be all too easy to sink into despair, to wallow, to curse the heavens. But that would not bring back Cerine. He needed to gather himself, needed to set about forming a reasonable plan.

Terryn and Ayleth, they would help. And Fendrel. And his father. He could not let things turn out as they had four years ago. He could not let Cerine be lost . . . or Fayline either.

Fayline's soul was still present in this world, not ousted to the Haunts. "It's possible," he said, grinding the words through his teeth. "She might yet be . . ."

His voice trailed away as something caught his eye under a pile of papers on his desk. A scrap of writing that he immediately recognized. Over the years, he had saved and pored over her many letters often enough to know Cerine's handwriting in a glance.

But this wasn't one of her letters. No, this scrap of paper was burned around the edges. When he drew it out from among the others in the stack, he half expected it to disintegrate. But it held together, and when he lifted it to his face, his eyes widened with horror as he realized what it was.

*A great poison will spread through the hearts of my people, giving rise to Falsehood reigning in the name of Truth. But I will send a champion. I will send the one whom I have chosen to cut off the head of deceit and lead the people back to Me. United in brotherhood, both shade-taken and un-taken will stand together, establishing a new legacy under My Name.*

How could this be? He had burned the whole book and scraped the ashes in the grate afterwards, leaving no trace of Cerine's heresies, nothing that could incriminate her, nothing that could lead her to the block. How had this scrap survived the flames?

And how in the Goddess's name had it ended up here

on his desk? Had this one page somehow flown free from the rest? Had Cerine in her frantic struggles managed to save it?

Or were there other powers at work in this world and determined that he not hide from the truth?

Gerard stared at those words, so close to the *Seion-Ebathe* he had been trained to recite while still in his cradle, and yet so dangerously different. His lips moved almost against his will, and he whispered: "*United in brotherhood, both shade-taken and un-taken—*"

The door opened.

Gerard slammed Cerine's writing down on the desk, hiding it under his hand. Then he rose from his seat, stepping back from the desk. "Uncle."

Fendrel stepped into the office and drew the door shut behind him. He had the look of a hunted animal about his eyes as he moved across the room toward Gerard. His arm was bound from the wound he had inflicted on himself in the ballroom, his face haggard after the exertion of his shade's power.

Gerard felt no sympathy. He observed Fendrel's gray face as he might observe the face of his nearest and dearest enemy. He held himself very straight and tall, refusing to be the first to break the silence between them.

Fendrel drew a long, ragged breath and finally spoke. "You have seen to your guests then, my Prince?"

"They have been sent away," Gerard said. "Venatrix Everild opened the barrier for a few hours late this morning. Even the pavilions have gone."

Fendrel's eyes roved up and down Gerard's figure. He still wore his wedding clothes from the night before, though he'd unfastened the doublet on one side, letting it fall open to reveal the silk undershirt. "Have you slept yet?" Fendrel asked.

Gerard shook his head. He was so exhausted, he feared one wrong step would send him crashing to the ground. But he knew that if he laid down his head, if he closed his eyes, he would only see Cerine's terrified face staring at him from over the edge of a knife. He would only hear Fayline's voice made hideous with heartbreak and hatred, each word she poured into his ear laced with betrayal.

No. He hadn't slept. He wondered if he would ever sleep again.

Fendrel sighed, his wide shoulders slumping suddenly, and he leaned his knuckles on the desk, resting heavily into them. Somehow, it seemed wrong for Fendrel to display even this momentary weakness. He was the Venator Dominus. The Black Hood. He was the hero of the Witch Wars. How *dare* he, after everything he'd done, reveal any vulnerability?

Gerard swallowed, grimaced, and looked away, fixing his gaze on his own hand, which still covered Cerine's scrap of writing. "What about Terryn?" he asked, his voice thick. "Has he awakened yet?"

Fendrel shook his head.

Well, at least someone was getting some rest. Though Gerard rather doubted Terryn's poisoned sleep was peaceful.

"What will happen to him?" he asked. "Can . . . can the curse be broken?"

A long silence was his only answer. Gerard scarcely dared to glance up at his uncle, not wanting to read his expression. He knew what Fendrel would say if he could find the words. The curse of the Warpwitch was supposed to have been broken. Twenty years ago, Fendrel himself had carved it out of Terryn's face. But now that effort had been proven ineffective, what did the future hold for Terryn? Could the curse be broken at all? Or was it too deeply planted? Would he live forever in the thrall of a witch?

No. Such a life was unacceptable. Certainly it was unacceptable within the Order of Saint Evander. If the curse could not be broken—truly broken this time—Terryn would be dealt the Gentle Death. And that would be the end of it.

"I summoned the Phasmatrix Domina," Fendrel said. "Several days ago, I sent a message. She will be here shortly. She will test Terryn then."

"You have to save him, Uncle," Gerard said.

Fendrel didn't speak.

"You have to do something," the prince persisted. "It's . . . it's Terryn."

"I know."

What more could be said? Fendrel knew what Terryn meant to Gerard. And Gerard knew all that Fendrel had planned for Terryn, he knew how vital Terryn was to every future scheme his uncle had in mind. The bond between the two of them—half-brothers who ought to have been fated enemies—had been of Fendrel's creation. Had Gerard's father had his way, Terryn would have been shipped back to Talmain at the end of the war, certainly not brought into the inner family circle, always trailing in Fendrel's footsteps, always thrown into company with the young prince.

Yes, Gerard thought bitterly, even that friendship was a mere fabrication forced on the two of them. Not exactly *against* their wills; simply *regardless* of their wills. Even so, the bond was mutually genuine and heartfelt.

The prince bowed his head, which suddenly felt too heavy. More out of a desperate need to change the direction of his own thoughts than anything, he asked, "And my father? How is he holding up through all of this?"

Fendrel raised his head and met Gerard's gaze, his eyes like two points of steel. "Your father is the reason I'm here. I've come to take you to him. It's time that . . ." He closed his mouth tight, as though trying to swallow his own words. His jaw worked, and the muscles in his throat moved painfully. "It's time that you knew the truth,

Gerard."

"The truth?" Gerard echoed, frowning. Unease writhed in his gut, though for no reason he could name. "What are you talking about?"

Again, Fendrel shut his mouth. This time he shook his head. Strands of pale hair escaped the tight braids holding them back from his face and fell in straggling wisps across his forehead. "It's better if I show you," he said.

Gerard wanted to argue. He was so sick of ambiguities, so sick of half-truths and games. As Fendrel straightened and started to turn toward the door, Gerard nearly stopped him with a sharp demand that his uncle, for once in his Haunts-damned life, simply tell him the truth.

As though hearing his nephew's silent tirade, Fendrel paused and looked back at him. Just a look, not a word. But there was something in his eye . . .

Gerard bit down hard on a curse. But he stepped out from behind his desk, leaving Cerine's scrap of writing where it lay. He followed Fendrel out of the office.

The halls of Dunloch were unnaturally quiet. Many of the household staff, Gerard knew, had fled along with the wedding guests, making their escape through the temporary opening in the barrier spell. The voices of the Siveline Sisterhood echoed from far away, off in the chapel where they sang over the dead body of Duke d'Aldreda, just as they had sung for his daughter less than a week ago.

Gerard expected Fendrel to lead him to his father's suite of rooms, which was no more than two turns from Gerard's own chambers. Instead of proceeding to the west wing, however, Fendrel took a back staircase down to the ground floor. They emerged, rather to Gerard's surprise, in the pillared hall just outside the long portrait gallery. Fendrel continued without pause, striding into the gallery, and Gerard hurried behind.

But the gallery was empty. No sign of the king anywhere.

"Uncle," Gerard barked, his voice echoing against the high ceiling.

Fendrel didn't stop or turn. He progressed purposefully along the gallery, beneath the eyes of those heroes, saints, and priestess-queens of old. He marched all the way to the gallery's end, where afternoon light from the east-facing windows revealed the faces of Queen Leurona and her infant son. When Fendrel strode ahead so that he looked as though he would walk directly into the painting itself, Gerard nearly called out to him again.

Before he opened his mouth, his uncle put out both hands, caught hold of the golden frame, and pulled. The tall image swung back on hinges Gerard had not realized existed, revealing a narrow doorway, a set of steps, and beyond . . . darkness.

Gerard, halfway down the gallery, stopped. After all the horrors of the night before, after all the revelations and all the fear, something like this shouldn't make his heart pound so painfully, until his pulse ticked under his jaw. But this was Dunloch. This was his home. He had been master here for the last five years. He thought he knew all the castle's secrets—every room, every passage, every attic and cellar.

How had he never realized what lay beyond that painting?

Fendrel paused in the doorway, looking back at Gerard. "Come," he said. "Your father is waiting." Then, turning his massive shoulders until they would fit through that narrow opening, he stepped through, descending swiftly out of sight.

A shock coursed through Gerard's limbs. Galvanized into motion, he hastened after his uncle, pausing in the doorway to try to see what waited below. The shadows were so dense, he could not even see Fendrel, though the older man could be only a few paces ahead. It was like stepping out of this world. Like stepping through a crack in reality into the unknown.

Did truth wait on the other side?

Gerard began the descent. Within three paces, he could scarcely see his own hand in front of his face. Within four, he could see nothing at all. He moved by feel and by sound; his hands slid along the cold walls crushing in close on either side of him, and his ears strained to catch the creak of Fendrel's boots up ahead.

"We had a saferoom created down here soon after the Witch Wars." Fendrel's voice sounded suddenly in front of him. Startled, Gerard nearly lost his footing. He pressed his hands hard into the walls, fingers tensed, holding himself upright.

Fendrel continued, his voice strangely casual, strangely

calm in contrast to the pound of Gerard's pulse: "I placed powerful blood wards around the door and the walls—wards that I reinforce every year to make certain they remain as strong as the day I set them. They prevent any but those of du Glaive blood from entering the chamber."

Gerard tried once or twice to answer before finding his voice. "Is this where my father hid last night during the attack?" No answer came, and Gerard followed up his question with another, spoken with more force. "Why wasn't I told about this place?"

Still no answer but the thud of boots on stone. Then, finally, "Watch your footing. The stair ends here. Turn left and follow me."

Was it his imagination, or were the walls closing in tighter? Gerard's breathing hitched, and he hastened down the last few steps more quickly than before, jarring his bones when he found no final step and his foot came down hard instead on level ground. He whirled to the left; his heart jumped with relief to see a gleam of light at the far end of a low-ceilinged passage. He couldn't gauge distance properly, but he didn't think it was far.

Between him and that light, Fendrel's shadow moved. Gerard hastened after him. Sooner than he expected, his uncle stepped into a doorway, his silhouette momentarily blocking most of the light before ducking through. Gerard, not wanting to be alone in the passage, picked up his pace. He stepped into the doorway.

He stopped.

Part of his awareness recognized the form of his father rising from a chair on one side of the room. He heard Guardin's voice exclaim, "No! Fendrel, no! What is he doing here?"

He heard his uncle answer, "It's time. He needs to know the truth. The whole truth."

But Gerard couldn't react to those voices, couldn't look at either of those men. His gaze, his mind, his entire awareness fixed on that which lay in the center of the room, spread out in funereal state on a slab of cold stone.

It was a headless corpse. An iron chain ringed its throat, but fresh blood seeped slowly from the wound—not a warm gush of life escaping, just a steady flow and gurgle that pooled around the body but never flowed over the edge of the slab, as though forever caught in a looping moment of time. The body itself was clad in what might once have been magnificent robes of black trimmed in gems, but now these were little more than burned tatters, and the bare arms crossed over the chest were likewise burned.

On a table, standing just a little apart from the slab, a head rested under a glass dome. Mouth agape. Tongue swollen, sagging, and purple. Eyes half closed. The skin raw and blackened, particularly the crown of the head, which was seared down to the skull.

Gerard knew who it was. He didn't have to guess; he didn't have to ask. He simply knew. Though everything within him insisted he must resist the knowledge, clamored for him to deny it.

Every impulse in his body exploded, telling him to flee, yet he stood in that doorway, hands grasping both sides of its frame, and could only stare.

"Come here, Gerard." Fendrel stood on the far side of the stone slab and beckoned. "Come and meet the Poison of Perrinion. Come and meet Dread Odile."

# CHAPTER 22

AYLETH BALANCED ON THE BACK LEGS OF HER CHAIR, her foot propped against the edge of Terryn's bed, her knee pulled up slightly as she watched him sleep. Still clothed in the rags of her ballgown, she cradled her wounded left arm close, trying to will away the pain.

No matter what she tried, no matter how she pretended, she could not will away the hurt she had seen flash through Laranta's spirit just before her shade was overcome by the iron poison and driven deep down inside her. In all the years of their strange, forced partnership, Ayleth had never used such cruelty to control Laranta.

Now this moment would always stand between them. Would they ever recover the natural ease of relationship they had once enjoyed?

Even to ask that question in the privacy of her thoughts was heresy.

What would Terryn say if he could read her mind? The question plagued her as she studied his unconscious face. Gerard had helped her carry him to his room last night, a task she could have done on her own with Laranta's aid, but which she could never have accomplished alone with her arm wounded and bleeding. After he helped her lay Terryn on his narrow bed, Gerard had said only, "Stay with him, Ayleth," before slipping out to deal with whatever it was princes must deal with under such circumstances.

Her prince had issued a command. So Ayleth stayed. The hours slipped slowly by, and blood from her three puncture wounds soaked through layers of hastily wrapped bandage torn from the hem of her ballgown.

She'd grabbed a spare cloak from among Terryn's belongings and draped it over her bare shoulders to keep from freezing to death. The gown itself would certainly never be used for dancing again; its once-voluminous skirts were little better than rags by now.

When he stirred, Ayleth's heart leaped. She slipped her foot off his bed, let the chair drop to all four legs, and leaned over Terryn, holding his cloak tight against her chest. His brow puckered, and his mouth twitched as though in pain. "Terryn?" she whispered. "Terryn, can you hear me?" On impulse, she reached out to take one of his hands. His fingers were so cold, but—

Her heart gave another lurch. His fingers had tightened on hers.

He didn't wake at once. His consciousness must ascend through many layers of poison, leaving his shade buried deep under suppressions. But he would recover consciousness soon, his body numb at first and then flooding with pain. Paralysis poisons never wore off easily, Ayleth knew from experience.

Well, if nothing else, she would be here for him when he opened his eyes. Odd . . . another smile pulled at her mouth. Even a few days ago, she never would have pictured herself in this position: seated beside Terryn's bed, holding his hand, waiting to offer support and comfort to this man who was her competitor.

What had the world come to?

She studied his face as his soul worked its way up toward wakefulness. Several weeks had passed since the last time she'd had opportunity to observe Terryn in his sleep. The first time happened after such short acquaintance that all she'd been able to see was her enemy lying before her. A handsome enemy, yes, but still an enemy. Someone to keep a wary eye on.

How could it be that such a change had come over these same features? Not the horrible, warping change she'd witnessed last night. No, this change was much more subtle and, in its way, more frightening. He looked vulnerable. He looked lost. He looked . . .

The long breath she drew shuddered in her throat. "Please, Terryn," she whispered. "It's time for you to wake up. Please."

His brow knotted. Did he hear her? She remembered too well what it felt like to come out from under the influence of the paralysis poison. She remembered being awake but unable to move even so much as an eyelid. Painfully aware of the world around her but unable to take part in it.

She leaned in closer, her face hovering just above Terryn's. Hesitantly, not entirely certain why she did what she did, she let go of the cloak and gingerly placed her left hand against his scarred cheek. The same cheek that last night she had seen blazing with the witch's sigil.

It was probably her imagination, but, despite Laranta's deep suppression, she thought she felt the pulse of ugly Anathema magic deep down under her palm. The curse was still present.

When he came to, would he be himself? Or would he be a witch's minion?

Ayleth squeezed his hand tighter, willing strength into his spirit. "Please, Terryn," she whispered. "I need you. There's no one else I trust. There's no one else who can help me help the prince. I need you to come back. I need you to—"

His eyelids fluttered. Then, uttering a groan that sent Ayleth's heart thudding, Terryn opened both eyes in a flash of brilliant, pain-laced blue. For a moment there was nothing but pain in his gaze. Then, with a few more slow blinks, his vision cleared, focused.

"Ay-Ayl—" He couldn't speak, of course. The poison didn't wear off that quickly. But he was back, and he was himself, and Ayleth could not stop the smile that burst across her face.

"Don't try to move," she said, moving her hand from his cheek to his chest. "It'll only frustrate you and slow the waking process. Just rest for now. You've had a wretched time of it, Venator du Balafre."

She felt his heart beating hard beneath her touch. While he'd slept, she had removed his once-elegant, now-shredded jerkin and shirt, hoping he might breathe more easily. Now she became suddenly aware of his bare skin under her fingers. She didn't pull away, however.

Terryn drew long breaths, the muscles of his face and neck tightening and relaxing and tightening again. Even with Laranta suppressed, Ayleth could sense the ripples of pain flowing through his spirit. He looked up at Ayleth again. There was something almost boyish, almost sweet in his perplexed gaze. It broke her heart.

His eyes begged her for information.

"You're cursed," she said simply. "By the Warpwitch. Just like Kephan. I don't know if it's a recent implantation or the old one from when you were a child. I saw her sigil burning through that scar of yours. I . . . I don't suppose you remember?"

He closed his eyes, as much of an answer as he could give in that moment. Then they flared open again, full of desperation, and she guessed what question his soul clamored to ask.

"Gerard is safe," she said quickly, squeezing the hand curled around hers. "The Warpwitch tried to make you hurt him, but you resisted as long as you could. You gave me time to interfere, and Fendrel took you down with a dart."

She went on to explain about the night's events, from the moment the Warpwitch revealed herself, housed in the Grand Mother's old body. Terryn's eyes never left her face the whole time she spoke. They widened slowly, and at one point she thought she saw a film of tears.

Only when she had finished, when her voice had trailed off to nothing, did he look away, staring at the wall beyond her with fixed intensity. A variety of expressions passed across his face, too subtle to be perceived by any but the keenest eye: fear, rage, confusion, shame.

Ayleth inclined her chin slightly. Hollis had told her stories of Dread Odile's reign, when witches ruled Perrinion. She'd told her about the way many witches took to collecting untaken mortals as "pets," treating them like beloved dogs, giving them shameful names, caressing them, loving them. Degrading them.

Ylaire had looked at this sweet blue-eyed boy as a giddy girl might look at a frolicking puppy. She'd taken him, tattooed her sigil into his skin, implanting a curse so deep that not even Fendrel du Glaive had succeeded in carving it out again. And now, years later, despite all he had done, all he had accomplished, she still owned him.

Terryn closed his eyes, breathing hard through his nostrils. Ayleth lifted her hand from his heart and sat back in her chair, feeling as though he had physically pushed her away. But she didn't let go of his hand.

"Can you . . . can you feel the curse now?" she asked quietly after some time had passed.

He glanced at her sharply, as though he'd forgotten

she was in the room. Then, with what appeared to be an incredible effort, he offered just the slightest shake of his head.

"You were probably commanded to forget it. Like Kephan," she said. She sucked in both dry lips, biting down as she considered her next words. He was at fault no more than Kephan had been. Kephan had nearly killed them both, but it wasn't Kephan himself who had willed their deaths. He was powerless against the curse inside him.

This most likely explained the oblidite anchor she'd found in Terryn's room, Ayleth realized. Terryn had found it while investigating rumors of the Phantomwitch, but something about the Warpwitch's curse on him had forced him to forget what he'd found, forget what he'd seen. He may have come close to catching both Ylaire and Inren several times over the last month, and he would never know it.

What could she say, though? What could she possibly offer him that would assuage the guilt even now wracking his soul? What hope or help was there for him? Fendrel himself had tried to remove the curse twenty years ago and failed. If he couldn't do it, who could?

A weight fell upon Ayleth's heart as she realized the consequences of Fendrel's failure. Because if Terryn's curse couldn't be removed, then . . .

There had to be way. She ground her teeth, curled her free hand into a fist. There *had* to be a way. In fact . . . there *was*. She knew it. She'd glimpsed it last night during the battle. She'd seen exactly how the curse could be broken.

Impulsively, she leaned over Terryn once more, pressing his hand between both of hers. Enough sensation had returned to his body by now that he felt it, and a spasm shot up his arm in response. He lacked control enough to pull his hand free, however, so she held on tight, ignoring the throbbing pain in her own wounded arm.

"You can be free of her curse, Terryn," she said.

She watched his face tighten. Did he know what she was about to say? His memories of last night must be vague at best, but did he remember what she had shouted into his ear while holding onto his spiny back? She saw the walls going up in his eyes.

"Your shade," she said, pushing on despite his resistance. "It can overthrow the curse. I saw it last night. I saw how strong it is, Terryn—unbelievably powerful! Not even Ylaire di Jocosa could fight it, not if you gave it ascendancy. Just for a moment."

His eyes and nostrils flared. If he could have summoned the strength to strike her, he would have. Anything to make her stop talking.

"I know you're afraid of it," Ayleth persisted. "You think it will destroy you the minute you relax your guard. But Terryn, you're wrong. I saw it. I *saw* your shade. It isn't what you think it is. It isn't vicious. Dangerous, yes, but it's not . . . it's not . . . ." She stumbled over the words, almost too afraid to speak them.

"It's not evil," she whispered.

The vein in his forehead bulged, and his dark skin flushed. The ice-cold fire in his eyes was enough to burn her, and it was all she could do to hold onto his hand, to meet his gaze, to fill her eyes with earnest entreaty, begging him to trust her, imploring him to understand.

His mouth moved. She leaned in closer, putting her ear to his lips as his cracked, tortured voice formed the words.

"He'll . . . kill you . . . *heretic.*"

It felt as if a poisoned knife had been stabbed into her ear.

Ayleth drew back quickly, releasing his hand, which fell lifeless to the bed beside him. She stared down at Terryn, stared down at this man who, only minutes ago, she had thought was no longer her enemy. She had thought he might even be her friend.

Bitterness rose in her throat like bile. What a fool she was!

She stood. Several answers churned in her brain, dagger-sharp words, but she couldn't make herself speak them. If she'd learned nothing else in these few, brief moments, let her finally take this one truth to heart: Venator Terryn du Balafre was not her friend. He never would be.

And he'd see her damned if she let her guard down even for a second.

She shut her mouth and walked from the room, slamming the door behind her. Leaving Terryn lying there. Alone in his slowly awakening body, alone to face the pain of the poison as it wore out of his system. She was done. Done. With him, with Fendrel, with the king, with the witches, with all of them.

With Gerard?

"Haunts damn, damn, *damn!*" she snarled, standing in the middle of a cold castle passage, clutching Terryn's cloak snug around her bare shoulders. She didn't even know where she was in relation to her own room. The many halls and stairways of Dunloch were unceasingly baffling to her senses. Like a lost soul, she turned this way and that, longing for escape, longing for a door through which she could run to her own freedom. Back to the forests, back to the mountains, back to the clear air and open country. Far, far from here, to a place where no one could tell her what to do with the spirit inside her, where no one could threaten her life for daring to speak against the Saint's teaching. Where no one could bind her, contain her, mold her into a shape she never was meant to fit.

But . . . what about the Golden Prince?

While she might hate all the others and everything they represented, she could never hate him. The Chosen King and the legendary Black Hood, they were just men. Cruel men, weak men, men driven by their own selfish agendas. But Gerard was more. Gerard was the Goddess's promise come to life.

And who was left to help him now? Who would battle these witches threatening his life and the life of his bride?

"Haunts damn," she breathed one last time. Resignation settled across her shoulders like a mantle. She knew then that she would never see Drauval again. She would never return to her forests; she would never return to her mountains.

"Inren and Ylaire are out there," she whispered, pulling her wounded arm close to her side and hurrying on down the narrow passage. She quickened her pace. "I will find a trace. I don't know how, but somehow, I will. And I will find Lady Cerine. As the Goddess is my witness, I will save her!"

But if she was going to do any of that, she sure as Haunts wasn't going to do it in a ballgown. The time had come to find her uniform, wherever they had stashed it. Her uniform, her weapons, her pipes.

The passage opened out into a wider hall, and when

she came to the end of this, she found herself at the top of the stairs leading down to the great entry hall. For a moment she froze, startled by a vivid memory of only the night before, when she had stood in this same place, clad in this same gown, gazing down these same stairs to where a tall, handsome figure in a red sash waited for her.

Ayleth gave her head an abrupt shake. That memory, she could not allow herself to keep. Glowering, she turned away from the stairs and continued toward the east wing, toward her own room. She knew she wouldn't find her uniform there, but perhaps Everild had left that pair of trousers and the undershirt behind. They would make a good start at least.

Ayleth entered the corridor and stopped abruptly. Someone stood down the passage, just outside what she believed to be her bedroom door. The day was growing late, and the only source of natural light in this corridor came from windows near the end leading to the east tower, but she saw at once that the man wore a hood.

A black hood.

She caught her breath. That sound, though slight, was just enough to draw his attention.

Fendrel du Glaive turned, and his iron eyes bored into hers across the little distance between them.

"Ayleth di Ferosa," he said.

A distant part of her mind realized he'd left off the "Venatrix" that was her title. She took a step back.

He turned to face her squarely, one hand upraised, fingers moving as though forming a spell she could not see without Laranta's shadow sight. "I am placing you under house arrest," he said. "I advise you to submit quietly."

"What?" Ayleth took another step back, then a third. Panic whipped through her veins. "What do you . . .? *Why?*" Her mind spun frantically. Had he overheard her conversation with Terryn just now? Or had Terryn somehow managed to speak to him between now and then? Was he arresting her for heresy?

"Resistance will be met with force," Fendrel said, and suddenly he was striding toward her, much too fast.

Ayleth whirled to run, the skirts of her gown flaring about her feet. She halted abruptly, face to face with a hideous, bloodied visage, and only after several blinks did she recognize Venatrix Everild, her nose broken during her encounter with the Phantomwitch, her face a mass of ugly bruises.

Before she could react, Everild moved. One heavy hand struck Ayleth across the face, knocking her clean off her feet. She hit the ground hard. The back of her head cracked against the floor, and the walls and ceiling spun. She tried to push herself back up, tried to regain control of her arms and legs.

Fendrel and Everild were both on top of her in a moment. Everild grabbed her shoulders and pushed her down to the ground, straddling her body so that she could only kick ineffectively at the air. Fendrel caught her by the throat with one hand, while with his other hand, he lifted a bottle to his mouth, grabbed the stopper in his teeth, yanked it loose, and spat it away. The fingers on her throat moved to her jaw, forcing her mouth open.

"Remember," Fendrel growled, holding the bottle over her face, "you brought this on yourself."

Dark, bitter liquid poured across her tongue. Ayleth choked, tried to scream, tried to spit it out in his face. Poison trickled down her throat, and there was nothing she could do to stop the darkness from closing in.

# EPILOGUE

DARKNESS.

Darkness all around. Whether she opened her eyes or closed them.

Darkness even down in her soul, which shuddered and quivered in terror while her body shuddered and quivered with cold and trauma.

Then, suddenly . . . light. Movement.

She gazed toward that bobbing glow as it approached, uncertain whether she looked upon her salvation or her doom. But at least it was something other than darkness.

A small figure seemed to manifest out of the shadows before her. A child, hardly more than three years of age, carrying a candle in her two tiny hands.

"Lady," she lisped, "you're awake?"

Cerine nodded slowly. She tried to speak, but her mouth was too dry, her throat too parched to utter more than a ghastly croak. She bowed her head and pressed her hands against her eyes, but only for a moment. Though the glare from the candle hurt, she craved its light, so she pulled her hands away again quickly and made herself look.

The child studied her through pale, round eyes. Behind her pupils, something moved. Cerine shivered as she realized the truth: This little one was a shade-taken.

When the girl opened her mouth to speak again, a strange voice moved through her lips: *"The witches are coming. They mean to hurt you. I'm sorry."*

The witches? Cerine tried to move, wincing as her wrists scraped against cold, tight manacles. Was she chained to the wall? Was this some sort of dungeon?

Arguing voices from the stairwell the child had

descended only moments ago drifted to Cerine's ears. Two vaguely familiar voices.

"I need a new host. This one is too old, too broken down. The girl you're keeping is young and strong, and she is un-taken. Her body will serve me well."

"No." The second voice was deep for a woman's and harsh as a forest of daggers. "You can't have her. *She* will not allow it."

"*She?* What say does *she* have? Are you not ascendant in this host of yours?"

"I am for the present," the harsh voice answered. "But if you make a move to harm her sister, she will overpower me again. She will suppress me, and she will kill you."

The first voice scoffed and spat. "She hates the girl. We all heard her at Dunloch. She wants to kill her for stealing the prince's affections."

"Yes," the harsh voice answered. "And no."

A long silence followed. At last the first voice uttered a foul curse, and the shadows in the stairwell flickered as though she threw up her hands in defeat. "Very well! We'll find some other host to serve me. In the meantime, what do *you*, Inren, wish to do with the little slut? We have no use for a pet at this time."

"I have an idea," Inren answered. "I am not yet sure, but I have an idea. First, however, I need you to tell me exactly what it was the little Seer saw in her vision-walking."

The two voices drifted back up the stairwell, fading at last beyond hearing. Cerine was alone again in the dark with the child and that which dwelt within the child. Her heart thundered in her breast as she gazed into those unnatural eyes.

"Will you help me to escape?" she asked.

The child shook her head slowly. "*No one can help you,*" the shade inside her answered. "*I have seen what is coming. I have seen what will be. No one can help you now.*"

# ABOUT THE AUTHOR

Sylvia Mercedes makes her home in the idyllic North Carolina countryside with her handsome husband, sweet baby-lady, and Gummy Bear, the Toothless Wonder Cat. When she's not writing she's . . . okay, let's be honest. When she's not writing, she's running around after her little girl, cleaning up glitter, trying to plan healthy-ish meals, and wondering where she left her phone. In between, she reads a steady diet of fantasy novels. But mostly she's writing.

After a short career in Traditional Publishing (under a different name), Sylvia decided to take the plunge into the Indie Publishing World and is enjoying every minute of it. The Venatrix Chronicles is her first series as an independent author, but she's got many more planned!

Don't miss the continuation of Ayleth's adventures in
Book 5 of The Venatrix Chronicles!

*Betrayal surrounds her on all sides,
and fiery doom awaits her at dawn . . . .*

# TEARS OF DUST

*Meanwhile be sure to read* Song of Shadows:

*Visit* www.SylviaMercedesBooks.com
*to get your free copy.*

Made in the USA
Middletown, DE
19 February 2020